Lilies That Fester

Also by Janis Harrison

Roots of Murder
Murder Sets Seed

Lilies
That
Fester

JANIS HARRISON

ST. MARTIN'S MINOTAUR   NEW YORK

www.minotaurbooks.com

Library of Congress Cataloging-in-Publication Data

Harrison, Janis (Janis Anne)
    Lilies that fester / Janis Harrison.—1st ed.
      p. cm.
    ISBN 0-312-28406-3
    1. Solomon, Bretta (Fictitious character)—Fiction. 2. Women detectives—
Missouri—Fiction. 3. Women gardeners—Fiction. 4. Gardening—Fiction. 5.
Missouri—Fiction. 6. Florists—Fiction I. Title.

PS3558.A67132 L55 2001
813'.54—dc21

                                                                2001041897

First Edition: November 2001

10   9   8   7   6   5   4   3   2   1

With much love,
I dedicate this book to my sister,
Gloria Walters.

Acknowledgments

This book was an emotional experience—writing about an issue that has plagued me all my life. Many people helped ease my journey as words gathered on the paper. I can't name you, but know that you hold a special place in my heart.

Perhaps you only smiled at me or gave me an encouraging hug. Maybe you redirected my thoughts for a few hours, talking about things that bothered you, taking me into your confidence. But most of all, you showed me that you cared. This helped "turn the page."

I treasure you, and call you "Friend" in the purest, most loving sense of the word.

—JANIS HARRISON

For sweetest things turn sourest by their deeds;
Lilies that fester smell far worse than weeds.

—excerpt from "Sonnet XCIV"

WILLIAM SHAKESPEARE

Lilies That Fester

Chapter One

❀ "Death hasn't diminished Chloe's beauty," said Robbee. "That silver-blue casket was a great choice, Bretta. Too bad her eyes are closed, because their fabulous color would mirror the finish."

I ignored him so I could study the funeral bier without distraction. As the florist in charge, I searched for any minute detail that was out of sync. A bank of floral tributes surrounded the casket and perfumed the air to an intoxicating level. Behind me two hundred empty chairs waited for occupants.

To my critical eye the bouquet on the left overpowered, but the traditional spray of flowers across the lower half of the casket was elegantly styled. The freesia's creamy color matched the satiny lining. The melon-pink tulips, royal-blue iris, and yellow daffodils were the right seasonal touch. It was April, and spring had blossomed in Branson, Missouri.

Robbee lowered his voice. "So young and so-o-o sexy. I had great plans for her, but now I'll have to turn my sights on someone else." He leaned closer. "Maybe someone older and more experienced."

His suggestive tone grabbed my attention. Before I lost one hundred pounds Robbee wouldn't have given me a second glance. I'd never be a skinny-minny, but I had a waistline, and I could cross my legs with ease. For someone who's never experi-

enced "thunder thigh syndrome" the latter might seem insignif-
icant. I knew otherwise. Sitting in a chair and having the option
of flinging one leg over the other is damned important.

I wore a blue T-shirt with the tail tucked under the waistband of my jeans. Since the room was ultracool to preserve the
condition of the flowers, I'd added a plaid flannel shirt. There
was nothing unique about my clothes and that's what thrilled
me. Gone were the polyester pants and oversized blouses that
had been the basis of my wardrobe.

The experts say it takes twenty-one days to develop a habit.
At forty-five, I'd had plenty of time to perfect a routine of
overeating. My new figure was almost two years in the making. Twenty-two months ago, I'd become a widow. These facts
were tightly woven into the fabric of my spiritual and physical
regeneration. Carl's death had raveled a portion of my soul
that could never be mended. Other areas had grown stronger
in his absence.

Robbee's breath stirred the curls near my ear. "You smell
wonderful, Bretta. Let's go—"

I didn't let him finish. My self-esteem could use a boost, but
not here and not now. "Shh!"

"Yes, Ms. Solomon," he said, clamping his lips tightly
together. He pretended to turn an imaginary key in an imaginary lock on his generous mouth. With an elaborate gesture,
he rolled the phantom key in his hands, then seductively
tucked it down the front of his shirt, taking great pains to
expose his chest for my appraisal.

I'd seen better, but it had been a while. At thirty-two,
Robbee's lean good looks paved the way for his brazen manner. His long brown hair was pulled into a ponytail and tied
with a strip of rawhide. He had more lines than a Broadway
actor, but I was immune to his prattle.

I shook my head at him. "With all the florists in Missouri, I don't know why I've been saddled with you for an assistant."

Before he could speak our "corpse" sat up. "I want out of this thing. I've laid here so long it's beginning to feel comfortable."

"That's not your spiel," said Robbee. "You're supposed to say, 'Welcome to the first annual Show-Me Floral Designers' Competition and Conference.' "

"I know what I'm supposed to say, but I need a break."

"Help her, Robbee," I said, nodding to the dearly departed, whose leg was draped over the edge of the casket.

Robbee folded his arms across his chest. "If I wait, the show's gonna get better." To prove his point, Chloe's dress inched higher, revealing a shapely upper thigh. He waggled his eyebrows. "See what I mean?"

The casket teetered on its stand. "Go," I said, "before she tips it over and we have a bona fide use for the damned thing."

He sighed but strode up the aisle. Once Chloe was safely standing, she smoothed her navy dress into place over her trim figure. Petite, fair-haired, and lovely summed up her physical appearance, but her personality was harder to define. Chloe is quiet and reserved in a group. With me, she acts as if she's found a surrogate mother.

At twenty-five, she's the youngest of the six competitors in our design contest and the most naive. Robbee's flirtatious smile had brought a rosy glow to her cheeks. I sighed. Anyone who thinks all male florists are gay should see Robbee in action. He could charm the pistil from a cactus flower.

But a person can take only so much frivolity, especially when that person is in charge of the first floral contest our association has held. I'd been asked weeks ago to be the coordinator. Scuttlebutt had it that my name had been nominated because I hadn't attended the St. Louis design semifinals and

3

couldn't flat-out refuse. I'd accepted the job because it was an excuse to get out of River City.

Since Carl's passing, I'd thrown myself into my flower-shop business with a vengeance. I needed a change of scenery, and the chance to visit Branson was too good to pass up. However, after a day and a half with a bunch of egotistical, competitive florists, I was beginning to doubt the wisdom of my decision.

I rotated my shoulders to lessen the stress. When this weekend was still in the planning stage, I was sure Robbee and I could handle making the display bouquets and setting up the contest area. Before I left home, I'd worried myself into issuing a last-minute invitation to the contestants to participate in the behind-the-scene preparation. From the moment they stepped through the hotel's doorway I'd heard rumblings of discontent, with my abilities as contest coordinator their biggest beef.

In a cover letter to all the contestants, I'd made it clear that the design categories would remain a secret until Saturday when the competition began. I wanted the premise to be interpretation plus ingenuity—creativity under pressure. Now it seemed that the pressure was on me to reveal those categories. So far I'd stood my ground but tension was high.

Today was Thursday. Tomorrow the festivities would commence. I'd thought the conference fee was rather high, but two hundred eager florists had signed on to be entertained as well as educated by guest speakers who had made a name in the floral industry. Add in the cost of lodging at this pricey hotel, and the weekend would be danged expensive. Since I had a major role in the production, I wanted to make sure my colleagues got their money's worth.

But for now, all work would have to cease. I was starving. I glanced at my watch. It was after two o'clock. No wonder.

As I walked to the back of the conference room, I saw some floral supplies that had been left on a table. "Janitor, mother, contest coordinator," I muttered as I swept the mess into my oversized handbag. "Is there no end to my duties?" The pint of flower preservative was a tight fit, but I squeezed it into my purse.

At the door, I called good-bye to Chloe and Robbee. Neither looked around. They lounged against the casket as if they were in a single's bar. Robbee was such a tease, I hoped Chloe wouldn't take him seriously. But that's not my problem, I told myself as I entered the lobby of the Terraced Plaza.

The hotel is a five-year-old structure of glass and concrete and is part and parcel of an estate known as Haversham Hall. The old residence, with its palatial gardens and unique botanical conservatory, sprawls across a bluff overlooking Table Rock Lake. The hotel, located at the base of the bluff, was built to accommodate the surge of organizations needing a place to hold their conventions since Branson had become a vacation hot spot.

Yesterday when I walked in the front door, I'd been tempted to tuck tail and scurry back to my car. For someone who's afraid of heights this hotel levitates my phobia to a new stratosphere. The structure is nine stories high and each floor has a balcony that circles the interior of the building. An adventuresome guest can step directly from her room and look over the railing to the lobby below or across the heart-stopping abyss to the opposite tiers of rooms.

Glass-enclosed elevators bob up and down the walls like fishing lures, beguiling would-be victims. Thirty-foot trees, festooned in clear twinkle lights, shade the lobby with an ambience that's congenial and refreshing. Brick planters filled with tropical foliage edge ramps that carry foot traffic to different levels or terraces. A lounge, a café, and a souvenir shop were tucked into alcoves. The floral conference had access to numerous meeting rooms on the ground floor with storage for the mass of donated flowers in the basement.

A formal restaurant topped the building, and I'd been told the view was breathtaking. Tonight I'd have my chance to witness this dramatic display when officers and contestants came together for the introductory dinner. But for now, I was happy to have my feet firmly planted on the lower level of the hotel.

I saw Alvin at the front desk and made a quick detour over to him. Before I went up to my room, I needed to see if my last contestant had arrived. Yesterday, Angelica Weston, or Gellie, as she's affectionately known, had car trouble on Interstate 44 just outside of Springfield.

Alvin's gaze was locked on a computer screen. A young woman hung over his shoulder. I stopped at the counter and heard the woman say, "If you can find a 'Mrs. Carol Salmon' registered, I'll quit harping at Daphne. But I still say she didn't try to deliver these messages. They've been on my desk since yesterday, waiting for me to do her work."

I figured Alvin hadn't seen my approach. I was wrong. Briefly he held up a pudgy hand. "Wait a second, Bretta," he said, then continued typing.

Alvin's official job title is "Hotel Event Specialist." He's in his thirties, with thick chestnut hair and skin the color of an unbaked biscuit. He looked as if he never did anything more strenuous than pecking the keyboard. He wore the hotel uniform—teal slacks and a white crewneck shirt. The knit material hugged his love handles like cream over a plump strawberry. I licked my lips. A gnawing hunger was taking over my brain—biscuit, cream, and strawberry.

In the past few weeks, I'd visited with Alvin a number of

times on the phone as we hashed out details for the floral contest. He'd listened to what I needed in the way of chairs, tables, refrigerated space for the donated flowers, huge trash containers, handy access to water, the casket from a local mortuary, and an ample supply of patience.

Alvin had met each of my demands and then some. It had been his idea to make optimum use of the hotel's banquet facilities by dividing the main meeting room, where we'd set up the funeral bier, from the actual contest area. For added drama, he'd suggested that the florists be asked to wait in the lobby and be admitted all at one time for the opening ceremony. That way Chloe wouldn't have to endure a lengthy stay in the casket before welcoming the visitors to the conference, and the attendees would have the full effect of the body in the casket as they made their way into the room. I was in agreement, so events were moving along.

Alvin finished typing and threw up his hands. "I give up. She isn't registered. In fact, there isn't anyone named Salmon here. I'd say toss the messages."

"I can't do that. The McDuffys are guests here. I'll just make a note that when they return, someone—named Daphne—has to let Vincent know the messages weren't deliverable." She peered at the slips of paper in her hand. "And everyone says my penmanship is atrocious."

She walked off muttering, and Alvin swiveled his chair to face me. His mouth curved into a welcoming smile.

"So," I said, leaning against the counter. "How's tricks?"

Alvin gave a mock shudder. "In this stellar hotel we avoid the use of that word."

I chuckled. "Just for the record, the service and your staff have been superb."

"Things are running smoothly?"

7

I thought of all the potential problems and sighed. "Let's just say that everything in *your* power is fine. I'm still a bit dubious about my part in this soiree." I gestured to the keyboard. "Could you tell me if Angelica Weston has arrived? She was supposed to be here yesterday, but she had car trouble. If she's stranded in Springfield, I need to know so I can rearrange my schedule and go get her."

Alvin clicked a few keys. "Yes, ma'am, she's here." He grinned. "See? Another worry resolved. You've got to have more faith, Bretta."

The telephone buzzed before I could give him my personal opinion of faith versus hard work, perseverance, and plain old bullheaded stubbornness. I waved farewell and moved on, giving the lobby a sweeping glance.

A good-looking man seated on one of the sofas peered at me over the top of an open newspaper. I got the impression he'd been giving me a thorough inspection. When I turned my attention to him, he met my gaze with a direct stare before raising the paper.

The brief glance we exchanged wasn't much, but I sucked in my stomach and wondered who I was trying to impress. I didn't recognize him as a fellow florist. He was simply an attractive man sitting in the lobby, but I'd responded to him like a flower taking up water after a drought. Confused by my reaction to a total stranger, I ignored the glass elevators, opting for the stairs.

It was a long climb to the fifth floor, but I needed the exercise. At the door to my room, I slipped the plastic card into the key slot, waited for the little lights to flash from red to green, and then turned the handle. The door met with a bit of resistance before swinging open.

What I needed was a cool drink and a snack. Before I left home, I'd fortified my suitcase for just such an occasion. I hauled my bag out of the closet and flipped back the lid to reveal my cache of goodies—diet style.

I groaned. "What was I thinking?" Fruit and fat-free cookies when I yearned for cashews in caramel or pecans in fudge. "Stop it. Think thin. Think chic." I savored a vision. "Chic . . . ken fried to a crusty, golden brown."

I passed over the apples and bananas and grabbed a peach. While munching the succulent fruit, I opened the draperies, taking care to stand a few feet away from the floor-to-ceiling window.

Haversham Hall had rounded out its tourist complex with a miniature golf course that was in the final stages of completion. The theme "The Wonders of Missouri" was played out in Lilliputian detail: a small-scale version of the St. Louis arch. From Mark Twain's *Tom Sawyer* a partially whitewashed board fence. A log cabin portrayed Laura Ingalls Wilder's *Little House on the Prairie*. A natural cave was rumored to be a real tourist treat, but it was the distant, natural view that inspired me.

The Ozarks were beautiful in the spring—miles and miles of country overlaid with trees. Stark branches were budded with nubs that would soon open and flourish under the warm Missouri sun. Cedar and pine spiced the vista with hope of life everlasting. White dogwoods looked as if they'd been caught in a freaky snowstorm, their four-petaled flowers bursting into a frothy cloud of bloom. Redbuds appeared like a rosy mist, rising from the earth, spreading color to a forest of greens and browns.

In crowded spots the trees rose tall and spindly, their limbs spaced farther and farther apart as they competed with their neighbors for room to grow. Others less pressed for space were compact; their limbs set at intervals that showed good nutrition as they maintained their correct cycle for maturity.

Breathing deeply, I allowed the true reason for this trip to surface. I'd come to Branson to get away from all that was familiar, so I could concentrate on what I wanted to do with the rest of my life—a life that didn't include Carl.

My flower shop in River City made me a good living and gave me an outlet for my artistry. I'd used Carl's life insurance money to buy an old mansion and was renovating it into a boardinghouse. I had friends. I had work. I had a fabulous home in the making. But I wanted—no—I needed more.

In the two years since Carl's death, I'd jumped from one project to another—always busy, always working, always on the move. I gave those tall trees another speculative look. Was I like them? Trying to reach new heights by stretching myself beyond limits that weren't healthy? During the next storm would I splinter because my foundation was weak from having tried to cover too much space in too short a time?

Carl had been a deputy with the Spencer County Sheriff's Department. He'd made me privy to his investigations—everything from assault to murder. My interest in his job and his trust in me had cemented our marriage as a partnership. Carl had used me as his sounding board by laying out the facts of a case he was working on. We'd discuss the evidence, and I'd point out possibilities or weak links. My lips twitched. Carl hadn't always agreed with my assessment—he could articulate with the best—but after I'd been right a few times, he'd listened to my theories and publicly given me credit.

After his death, I'd been drawn into doing some amateur

sleuthing on my own, which had almost gotten me killed. Abruptly I turned from the window and tossed the half-eaten peach into the trash.

The afternoon sunlight streamed into my room and high-lighted a five-by-seven manila envelope lying on the floor by the door. I hadn't noticed it when I walked in. My mind had been on food.

Before picking up the envelope, I pushed a portion of it under the door. Tight fit, but I figured that's how it had been delivered. A note had been taped to the outside, and when I caught sight of the salutation, my eyebrows winged upward in surprise. It had been twenty-two months since anyone had referred to me as:

Mrs. Carl Solomon:

Last month my wife and I were in your shop buying flow-ers for our daughter's funeral. A nice lady helped us with our order because you were on the phone. We shamelessly eaves-dropped on your conversation and learned that you would be in Branson this weekend for a floral convention. We've timed our trip to coincide with this event.

Your husband, Deputy Carl, was a fine man and a thoughtful officer. My wife and I live in the outer reaches of Spencer County, and when he was on patrol, he would stop in and visit with us. He often spoke of you and told us how you helped him with some of his investigations. We've since read in the River City Daily *that you were instrumental in assisting the sheriff's department in solving two murders.*

We don't have enough evidence to take to the authorities. You, Mrs. Solomon, are our only hope to right a terrible wrong. Please keep this envelope safe for us. If we haven't

*retrieved it by 7:00 A.M. on Friday, you have our permission
to open it and assess its contents.*

> *Our highest regards,*
> *Vincent and Mabel McDuffy*
> *Spencer County, Missouri*

Chapter Two

✤ "McDuffy?" I murmured thoughtfully. The name jingled a bell of recognition. I picked up the phone and punched in the number for the front desk. "This is Bretta Solomon in room 521. I think you're holding some messages for me from Vincent McDuffy."

The woman's voice was cool. "The notes we have are addressed to a Mrs. Carol Salmon."

"I know that's what it might look like, but I found another message in my room from Mr. McDuffy. I'm Mrs. *Carl Solomon* from River City, Missouri. Will you please have someone deliver those messages to me immediately? Thank you."

Carl had talked about several families he regularly saw while out on patrol. My gaze landed on the fruit in my suitcase. Peaches? Peach pie had been one of Carl's favorite desserts. I'm only a so-so cook, and a flaky crust isn't within my realm of expertise. But it seemed to me that a *Mabel McDuffy* had sated Carl's sweet tooth with slices of pie when he dropped in for a visit.

As for their daughter's funeral service, I didn't recall a single detail. Last month had been hectic what with getting the fine points ironed out for this conference.

I was prepared with a tip and the note from Vincent when I

opened the door to the same woman who'd been at the desk with Alvin. She frowned when she saw me. "Hi," I said cheerfully. "Sorry about the mix-up, but I didn't realize those messages were for me until I got to my room." I held out the paper that had been taped to the envelope so she could see Vincent's writing. "It is atrocious penmanship."

She saw the scrawl and visibly relaxed. "My name's Helen. Thanks for calling down. This really takes a load off my mind. The messages seemed rather urgent, and I didn't want to be responsible for not getting them to the right party."

I took the offered slips of paper, then held out the money, but she shook her head. "No thanks. I'm just glad we got this straightened out. Mr. and Mrs. McDuffy are the sweetest people. In the last four days, they've become very special to me."

"Four days, huh? They must be enjoying all the sights."

She shook her head. "Nope. Most of the time they sit in the lobby or take the shuttle up the hill to the conservatory. They're a devoted couple, always holding hands. Mrs. McDuffy isn't well." Helen leaned closer. "I think she has cancer. She wears a gray wig and is as thin as a wafer. I feel sorry for them. They lost their only child last month."

I was amazed at the extent of her knowledge of the McDuffys. "With so many guests, how in the world do you know all this?"

"I get bored, and Mr. McDuffy likes to talk." She gave a depreciative gesture. "I do, too. We hit it off."

"So where are they now?"

"I'm not sure. Their names aren't on the list for the shuttle. And I know they aren't in their room. I just talked to Carolyn, who cleans their floor, and she said they weren't there. They must have left early this morning because I came to work at seven, and I didn't see them go out."

I'd gone to the basement about 6:00 A.M. to unpack containers and get the mundane chores done so the designers could swoop in and do their thing. It must have been after six and before seven when the McDuffys pushed the envelope under my door.

I got the impression that Helen would have stayed and talked longer, but I was curious about my messages, so I cut short our visit. I waved the slips of paper. "Thanks," I said, easing the door closed. "When I see Vincent and Mabel, I'll be sure to tell them how conscientious you were."

As soon as the latch clicked shut, I started reading, or perhaps I should say, deciphering Vincent's handwriting. I could see how Helen had thought she was looking for a *Mrs. Carol Salmon*. Each note was headed with the greeting: Mrs. Carl Solomon.

Wednesday—11:00 A.M. Please contact me. I'm a guest here in the hotel.

Vincent McDuffy.

Wednesday—7:00 P.M. Please call our room immediately. My wife and I need to speak with you.

Vincent and Mabel McDuffy.

Wednesday—10:00 P.M. We can't wait any longer. I'm sorry our paths didn't cross, but we're placing our trust in you, based on your husband's faith.

Vincent and Mabel McDuffy.

I swallowed the lump that rose in my throat and wondered what my loving husband had spilled to these people. But more importantly, what were they expecting from me?

Helen had said the couple wasn't in their room, but I needed info. I went to the phone and dialed my business in River City. While the number rang, I picked up the manila envelope. It was flat except for a hard rectangular box that might be a—

"The Flower Shop," answered Lois.

"Hi, it's me. Got time for a chat?"

"Yeah, if you hang on a minute."

The receiver plunked against the counter. Background noise told me she was finishing with a customer. Lois Duncan is my top designer, but she's more than an employee. She puts up with my quirky personality and quite simply—me.

In the last six months, I've tried Lois's patience further by my amateur sleuthing. Sid Hancock, the sheriff of Spencer County, uses a colorful array of words when he describes my active interest in the crimes of *his* county. Regardless of what Sid thinks, I've never gone looking for trouble, but I've always been more comfortable helping others with their problems than dealing with my own.

"Here I am," said Lois. "How's the vacation?"

Jerked back to the present, I gasped. "Are you kidding? Vacation? I'm working my fingers down to stubs."

"Have you met any unattached males?"

A mental picture of the man in the lobby flashed through my mind. "No. I'm still footloose and fancy-free."

Lois grunted. "You can put a stop to that if you'll wear your new black dress tonight. You did pack it?"

I looked across the room to the open closet door. Lois had gone shopping with me, and I'd let her talk me into buying the dress—tight skirt, nipped-in waist, and low neckline. "Yeah. It's hanging alongside that obscene nightie you hid in my suitcase. This isn't a seduction trip. I'm here to conduct a floral contest."

"Combine business with pleasure, and you'll come home fulfilled."

"Why do you think a man will solve my problems?" Before Lois, a happily married woman, could answer, I quickly said, "We're getting off track. I called to pick your brain."

Lois sighed. "We've been busy so there isn't much left to scavenge."

"Can you think back to last month? We did the funeral flowers for the daughter of Vincent and Mabel McDuffy. Do you remember waiting on them?"

"Sure. Their daughter's name was Stephanie, but they called her Steffie. She was only twenty-seven when she died."

"What was wrong with her?"

"Heart attack."

"At twenty-seven? That's terrible. It must not have been a big service or I'd have remembered."

"It wasn't. At the time I commented that it was a shame such a young woman had so few flowers."

"What do you remember about her parents?"

Lois sighed. "Bretta, I don't mind playing twenty questions, but before this conversation comes to an end, you will me tell what's going on?"

I grinned. "I wouldn't have it any other way."

"Yeah, right. The mother, Mabel, has cancer and had been taking chemo. She looked like a scarecrow with half the stuffing knocked out. However, the father, Vincent McDuffy, was huge. They're a 'Jack Sprat' in reverse. Surely you remember him, as obsessed as you are with weight."

"I'm not obsessed, just careful. You would be too if you'd

17

lost the equivalent of another person and still craved chocolate and fried chicken." I touched the brown envelope beside me. "The McDuffys are here in Branson. I found a note from them under my door, and three more at the front desk."

"Sounds like they're persistent. What do they want?"

"I'm not sure. Apparently when Carl was on patrol, he'd go by their house and visit. I think Mrs. McDuffy is the one who used to bake him pies."

"That's nice, but not enlightening. What's the rest of the story?"

"I wish I knew. In one of their notes they said something about me 'righting a wrong.'"

Lois snorted. "Well, that's up your alley. Did they say what this 'wrong' is?"

"No. I've been busy with conference duties, and we've missed connections."

"How did they know you were in Branson at that particular hotel?"

After I'd explained about the eavesdropping, Lois said, "I don't like this, Bretta. Why were they listening to your plans while ordering the flowers for their daughter's funeral? Sounds pretty weird to me. I'd keep my distance if I were you."

"I can't do that. Carl liked them, and they thought enough of Carl to trust me with this package."

"Package? What package? You said notes."

I laughed. "It's just an envelope with what feels like a small rectangle box inside."

"Is it making little tick-tick sounds?"

"You watch too many movies."

"No need for movies when I work for you. I get all the excitement I can handle."

"Then if I need some information, you won't mind nosing around?"

"Around where? Here in town?"

"Yeah. I've got this feeling—"

"See?" said Lois. "That's just what I mean. Your *feelings* scare ten years off of my life."

"Don't worry—yet. I'll talk to you tomorrow."

I put the receiver back in the cradle, then reread the McDuffys' letter. My uneasiness came from their mention of my role in solving two murders. Why bring that up? Why wouldn't the McDuffys come back for the envelope? Why would I need to "assess" the contents? My fingers traced the outline of the hard rectangular box. It felt like a cassette. Had they recorded a message for me? Was I being ridiculous?

There probably wasn't any need to get worked up over what could be nothing. This was another prime example of how I get sucked into other people's problems. It was much easier to contemplate the ands, ifs, and buts of the McDuffys than it was to mull over my own situation.

I placed a call to their room. There wasn't any answer, which bothered me since they hadn't been seen all day. That was surely odd since Helen had said that for the last four days Mabel and Vincent had spent their time in the lobby or taking the shuttle up to the conservatory.

I tempered my uneasiness by telling myself that they would be by in the morning to get the envelope. However, they'd asked me to keep it safe. I looked around for a hiding place. I was usually pretty good at this kind of thing, but a hotel room offered few choices. I'd had better luck concealing the bulky notebook that held the information for the contest. My notes and the compact disc that was the "key" to the contest were safely tucked away from prying eyes in the silver-blue casket that was on prominent display in the conference room.

I'd never examined the construction of a casket until yesterday. Chloe had told us the mattress was as thin as paper. Robbee had remarked that funeral homes rarely get complaints. I'd investigated the bottom of the stainless-steel box and found a metal grid supporting the flimsy pad. The space beneath the framework made a perfect place to hide my notes, but it wouldn't work for this envelope. It had to be here in my room.

After a moment's deliberation, I dropped the package behind the armoire, where it caught on a ledge and blended with the woodwork. I'd have to get down on my hands and knees to retrieve it, but I'd done as requested.

Now what was I to do? It was too early to get ready for the introductory dinner, an event I thought unnecessary. Those involved knew enough about each other to turn the gathering into a no-holds-barred bashing. Since I might be at the center of a major controversy concerning the design categories, I decided to make myself scarce until the appointed hour, but I could call Gellie.

I had reached for the phone when someone knocked on my door. I opened it with a flourish, thinking it might be the McDuffys.

In the hall was Effie, the secretary of the Show-Me Floral Association. I looked down into her rheumy blue eyes and smiled. A spry seventy-one, though her shoulders were stooped from fifty years of floral designing, she still maintains a forty-hour workweek at her flower shop.

"Are you busy, dear?" she asked, then smoothed her orchid dress, which picked up the lavender highlights of her hair. "I don't want to be a bother."

"You could never be that," I assured her. "I was going to call Gellie's room to see if she'd like to get together for a chat."

"Then she's arrived?" When I nodded, Effie sighed. "Well, thank goodness. Car trouble on an interstate is horrible. Zoom. Zoom. Zoom. Everyone in a rush, but no one willing to stop and help." Her chin came up. "Did I tell you about the woman who almost bashed my car yesterday when I arrived at the hotel?"

I nodded. I'd heard the story several times, and with each rendition, Effie had gotten upset all over again. Hoping to ward off a rise in her blood pressure, I gestured to the leather-bound binder in her hands. "Are you on a fact-finding mission?"

"I'm about 'facted' out, if there is such a word."

I heard a note of fatigue in her voice and studied her with concern. I'd always had a soft spot for little old ladies, which probably stemmed from a cruel fate that had snatched my own grandparents away before I'd gotten to know them. When I saw the tired droop to Effie's stooped shoulders, I asked, "Are you okay? Do you need to lie down?"

Effie grimaced. "After I make the place cards for tonight's dinner party, I might take a nap. I have a headache from my meeting with Tyrone." She peered up at me. "Do you know the Greek origin of the name 'Tyrone'?"

This was just one of the reasons I loved Effie. I couldn't always track which path her mind was taking, but the journey was usually interesting. "I haven't a clue," I answered.

Effie dabbed her watery eyes with a lace-edged hankie she pulled from her dress sleeve. "I find names fascinating, especially once I get to know the owner. Each generation has a trend, but most names have a historical foundation." Her brow furrowed thoughtfully. "I can't decide if fate decrees us a name because our personality has been defined before we're born, or if we subconsciously try to live up to the moniker we were blessed with at birth."

Airily, she waved the hand holding the hankie. "No matter. Last year, after Tyrone was elected president of the Show-Me Floral Association, I looked up his name in a book I'm partial to and found that Tyrone means 'ruler.' Most apropos considering his high-handed tactics at being involved in every aspect of his board's duties. Bernice is with him now. Allison has been summoned to appear at five."

I didn't know what Effie was talking about as to "historical foundation" and "fate decrees," but I identified the names "Bernice and Allison" and tried not to scowl. As treasurer of the association, Bernice's job is to make sure all the conference committees don't go over budget. To hear her talk, we're a bunch of willy-nilly spenders, and she's the only one who knows how to balance a checkbook.

Allison Thorpe is the association's vice president. In our hometown of River City, Missouri, Allison and I own rival flower shops. Our tedious relationship is like the back roads that wind their way through the Ozarks—pitted and pocked as a lotus pod.

I'd already accepted the job of coordinating the design contest when I learned Allison would be working on the conference, too. I'd been dubious, but so far we'd stuck to our individual responsibilities, having little personal contact.

"Tyrone hasn't asked me any questions," I said, studying Effie's wrinkled face. "Is that good?"

She winked charmingly. "You're doing an excellent job coordinating the designers' competition, dear. Even the 'ruler' couldn't fault your talents."

"I wasn't angling for a compliment, but I didn't realize

Tyrone was watching everything so closely. He's spent most of the time in his room."

Effie beckoned with a gnarled finger, and then led the way over to the railing. "It wasn't by chance that Tyrone was assigned the suite that looks directly down on the entrance into the conference area. Make no mistake, he knows what's going on."

I turned my attention to the second floor. As if on cue, the subject of our conversation appeared in the doorway of his room. Tyrone had an uncanny resemblance to Clark Gable—slim, debonair, neatly trimmed dark mustache. As I watched, he ran a finger over his upper lip, then tipped his head to look directly at me.

His sensuous gesture sent an unexpected jolt of heat across my skin. I was caught off guard since I didn't particularly like the man. First the stranger in the lobby and now Tyrone. What was wrong with me? Was I headed for some kind of health crisis?

Effie tapped my arm and nodded to the terrace lounge. She indicated two women sipping drinks. "I had three reasons for stopping by, dear. Delia and Miriam are two of them. They could be contributing more to our conference, but they're too busy figuring out a way to make you reveal the categories."

I studied the design contestants. I didn't know Delia particularly well, but to my way of thinking, she was hanging on to her youth by the tips of her fake red fingernails. In her late forties, she worked diligently to appear thirty—skintight blue jeans, bare midriff, spiked heels, and hair bleached so often it was as brittle and frizzy as a dandelion gone to seed.

Miriam and I went back years, but only in a casual way. At fifty-six, her translucent complexion is that of a natural redhead, her husky voice an even blend of confidence and arrogance. I get along with her, but only if I stand my ground. Her overbearing manner has a way of chafing tender areas.

"You said you had three reasons for coming by. What's the third?"

Effie rose on the tips of her sensible shoes and leaned over the banister. "He's seated over by the bar."

I grabbed her dress tail. "Good lord, Effie. Don't do that. What if you got dizzy?"

"I'd make a very small splat, dear."

At my insistence, she moved away from the railing. Once we were safely at the door to my room, she said, "Since you won't look, I have to tell you that Darren is drinking rather heavily."

"He's an artist. Perhaps he needs to unwind. A drink or two won't hurt, as long as he's sober for the competition."

Effie, a proper spinster, gave a disapproving sniff. "He isn't unwinding, dear. The origin of his name is uncertain, but it's believed to mean 'great one.' I think he's feeling the burden of performing before his peers."

I found that hard to swallow. Darren regularly flies to Europe to hold international design classes. His creative genius was responsible for all the flower designs used at the past two Missouri governors' inaugural balls. His achievements have been featured in several national magazines.

When Darren entered this competition, I was amazed that he'd waste his time on such small potatoes. He'd confided to me that he didn't care about winning, but was willing to lend his name to the contest. Sponsors had leaped at the chance to have their products touted by him. Money for second and third prize was a tidy sum. But the grand prize—an all-expenses-paid trip to Hawaii—made me wish I had a stake in the outcome.

I was ready to make my point to Effie, but she had her own opinion. She lowered her tone to a gossipy level. "I'm not sure how much you know about the situation, but Darren began his florist career as a delivery boy for Delia's shop. From what I understand, she challenged Darren to enter a contest, such as the one you're conducting, dear, and his hidden talent was discovered. It isn't helping the situation that Delia has spent the day complaining."

Effie imitated Delia's squawky whine to perfection. " 'I don't know which is more contemptible. Darren, for never giving my shop any recognition, or Hubert, for leaving without proper notice.' "

She rolled her eyes. "Of course, Hubert recognized which side of his bread had the jelly. I don't blame him for leaving Delia's employment. Why be her gopher when he had the chance to travel the world with Darren?"

Having dumped everything into my lap, Effie heaved a sigh. "I thought you should know what's going on. The gist of it is jealousy and resentment on Delia's side. Darren will only compound the situation with his excess use of alcohol." She patted my arm. "I'll be in my room if you need me, dear. Enjoy your visit with Gellie."

Oh, sure. Like I could enjoy a carefree chitchat with an old friend when one of my contestants was drinking himself into oblivion and two others were plotting against me.

Chapter Three

🌿 I didn't figure I'd get anywhere with Delia or Miriam, but I might be able to coax Darren into having a cup of coffee with me. I left my purse on the bed, but grabbed my door key and stuffed it into my pocket. I hesitated at the phone. I needed to touch base with Gellie, but the situation with Darren spurred me out of my room and down to the end of the hall.

I opened the stairwell door, took a few steps, then stopped. Someone was coming fast and furious from above. I plastered myself against the wall and waited. Zach, the other male contestant, came into view. He was dressed in green jogging shorts and no shirt. I gulped when he stopped a few feet from me.

"Don't wanna get too close," he said. "I've worked up an unpleasant aroma."

In my opinion there wasn't *anything* unpleasant about Zach. His muscles were like sculptured stone buffed to perfection. He wore a gold hoop in his earlobe, and the tattoo of a bumblebee decorated a patch of flesh above his heart.

I'd made the mistake of telling Lois that I looked forward to working with Zach. She'd put her own spin on "working." Her risqué comment came back to me, and I couldn't meet his friendly gaze. My roving eyes settled on the low ride of his shorts. Surrounded by a mat of black hairs, his navel made a cute little dimple that winked at me.

"You exercising, too?" Zach asked.

I dragged my gaze up to his face. "I . . . uh . . . hate those glass elevators. I take the stairs whenever I . . . uh . . . need to change floors."

Zach did a couple of deep knee-bends. "I'll see you tonight at dinner. Gotta go or I'll get stiff." He tossed me another smile before trotting off down the stairs.

I closed my eyes and rubbed the goose bumps on my arms. Lately I'd experienced flashes of heat, irregular heartbeats, and a frequent flutter in my stomach. I would class my symptoms as a massive case of nerves, except seeing Zach in those skimpy shorts had put images in my brain that hadn't been there in almost two years.

"What's the matter with me?" I muttered.

"A bad case of hormones, Babe."

My eyes flew open. "Carl?" I whispered.

Since his death, Carl's voice often plays in my head. Sometimes the tone is so clear and distinct I feel I can turn and see him standing at my side. He's most vocal when I'm trying to work out a problem, and his sage advice has helped me through some rough times.

I've never told anyone about hearing Carl's voice in my head. I knew I was hanging on to the remembered sound like a child does his favorite blanket. It comforted and helped ease the pain of being alone. I wasn't ready to give up Carl's memory, but a few weeks ago, I'd removed the wedding band from my finger. For twenty-four years it had adorned my hand, reminding me of the love and trust we'd shared.

A wave of sadness brought the threat of tears. I clenched my jaws. Get a grip. There wasn't time for sorrow or self-pity. This conference and competition were going to happen, and I'd better get my act together.

I stomped down the stairs muttering to myself. There was plenty to occupy me, and regardless of the physical signs, I was master of my own destiny. My body wasn't about to dictate any terms.

"It's time to get on with life, Babe," Carl reminded me softly.

I flung open the stairwell door and snapped over my shoulder. "I'm trying. Please don't nag." I turned around and there stood Chloe.

She blinked in confusion. "Sorry, Bretta, but I haven't said anything . . . yet."

My lower lip pooched out, and I blew a jet stream of air that blasted the bangs off my hot forehead. "Were you looking for me?" I asked.

"I saw you leave your floor and knew you'd be using the stairs." She twirled a blond curl nervously. "I wanted to ask you about the design categories."

"What about them?"

She took a deep breath and said in a rush, "I've never done competition before, and I'm worried I'll make a fool of myself."

I touched her lightly on the arm. "I've seen your work. You'll do fine."

"You really think so?"

"Sure I do. Besides, look at what you've accomplished already. You're in the finals. That took talent."

"Robbee says the same thing only with more coo and goo." She made a face. "A woman would have to be desperate to take him seriously." Her chin came up. "And I'm most definitely not desperate."

"Good for you," I said, moving away. Having caught sight of Darren, I added under my breath, "Looks like I've got another hand to hold."

The famed designer didn't give the appearance of a man riding a wave of success. Five empty beer bottles were lined up in front of him. His tall, lanky body was slumped against the table.

At his elbow was Hubert, who always wore black and loomed like a shadow. Hubert was past retirement, and from the expression on his face, wished he was anyplace but here. It was obvious that he'd tried to convince Darren to stop drinking. Frustration had driven the older man's slender fingers through his gray hair, making it stand out from his head like barbs on a cactus.

Hubert had spotted me and nodded toward Darren. "It's your turn," he mimed before scurrying off.

I smothered an expletive and strode purposefully across the lobby. I'd been lucky enough to be present when Darren had aced his first contest. I'd witnessed the creation of his winning design—five yellow roses, some willow branches, a watermelon, and three Granny Smith apples. He'd carved swans from the apples, placed them on a sculptured melon lake, and dramatically added flowers with the branches to create a contrived bouquet that was unique as well as whimsical.

As I approached Darren's table, I was relieved to see Delia and Miriam had left the terrace lounge. This conversation would go better without their catty remarks. But the handsome man I'd noticed earlier in the lobby was seated at the bar. He saw me and took the newspaper off the stool next to him. It was an open invitation, and my steps faltered. A quick glance around the room showed several attractive women, and I wondered why this man had set his sights on me. His attention was flattering, but I was out of practice in the art of flirtation. He nodded to the stool. I quickly shook my head before taking the chair opposite Darren.

Five beers would have put me under the table, but Darren focused on me, and for a second I was lulled into hoping that Effie and Hubert were worrywarts. Then he opened his mouth.

"Hey, sweet cakes. How's 'bout a beer?"

By no stretch of the imagination am I a "sweet cakes" kind of gal. The guy was soused. "No thanks. Aren't you celebrating a bit early?"

"I'm checking out." He waved an arm and nearly toppled out of his chair. "Atmosphere sucks."

While Darren recovered his seat, I summoned a waiter and ordered a pot of coffee. "Can you ignore it?" I asked. So there would be no misunderstanding, I tacked on, "Or them?"

He sat up straight and concentrated on forming each word, as if he could see what his lips were doing. "Don't need them. Don't need anyone."

I leaned forward and reached around the tidy row of brown bottles to place my fingertips on his arm. "But this contest needs your talent."

"I drink to my competition." He flicked each bottle with a thumbnail. "Chloe, the ingenue. Miriam, the self-serving witch. Delia, the blond bitch. Zach, the body beautiful. And finally, Gellie, the princess of pork."

I bristled. Gellie was overweight, but she didn't deserve this crude assessment. Before I could come to her defense, Darren spoke in a venomous tone. "Interfering twit."

Drunk, disorderly, and abusive. I couldn't deal with this on top of everything else. I got up and turned to leave, but Darren grabbed my wrist. "Need me? Never." His eyes narrowed. "Need my name? You're damned right you do."

My cheeks burned as I hurried to the elevator. I wanted escape and this was the closest, fastest way possible. Gellie's room was 418, and I headed straight for her. I was in need of a massive dose of her quick wit.

I punched the UP arrow, and the door swooshed open. I stepped into the glass-fronted box, keeping close to the wall and averting my eyes from the lobby, where the floor would disappear as I soared to dizzying heights.

Just as the door was about to close, the man from the bar ambled in. He gestured to the control buttons. "What floor?"

"Four," I said, my thoughts on Darren. He was right. I did need him and his name. What if he quit the competition? I had sponsors making huge donations because he was participating in the contest. Would I have to give back the money and the merchandise?

"Are you another butterfly enthusiast?" asked the man across from me.

Not an odd question since our florist convention wasn't the only one being held in the hotel this weekend. The Missouri Order of Butterfly Watchers had fluttered in yesterday complete with posters and pamphlets. From snatches of conversation, I gathered the group was soliciting new members to help plot the migrating trail of a bevy of egg-laden creatures.

"I'm with the floral convention," I said.

He chuckled pleasantly. "Butterflies and flowers. Sounds like the right combination." He held out his hand. "My name's Bailey Monroe, avid gardener and butterfly tracker."

I slipped my hand into his and tried to smile. "Bretta

Solomon, florist." To myself I added, "And soon to be a patient at the nearest psychiatric ward."

The bell dinged, and the door slid open. As I pulled my hand out of his, Bailey said, "Elevator's too efficient. I was working up the nerve to ask you to dinner so we could compare notes on what attracts butterflies to flowers."

It was a sweet pickup line, and caused me to take a closer look at him. He stood about six feet two. His dark hair was lightly frosted with about fifty years of life's trials and tribulations. Brown eyes crinkled with humor. A jaw that was square and strong gave the impression that he could be stubborn, or perhaps merely determined.

I stepped out of the elevator, but turned to say, "I'm busy with conference duties tonight."

"I'll make it a point to see you again," he promised as the door slowly closed.

Instead of going up, the elevator went down, and I was left with the feeling that I'd been escorted to the fourth floor. I watched Bailey return to the lobby and smiled. It certainly didn't hurt my ego that this handsome man had gone out of his way to meet me.

I walked down the hall, keeping close to the rooms and away from the railing that was a forty-foot drop to the ground floor. Maybe I should take up butterfly watching, especially if Bailey was an example of the membership. Even discounting the man's charm, chasing fertile butterflies sounded uncomplicated compared to what I faced this weekend.

My thoughts returned to my conversation with Darren. He'd been on the money with Zach. The man was most definitely body beautiful. Calling Miriam a "self-serving witch" was accurate. As was his assessment of Chloe and Delia. But

Gellie, most assuredly, didn't deserve the crude title "princess of pork." The memory of Darren's tone, when he'd called her an "interfering twit," troubled me.

I stopped at room 418. A tray by the door held the remnants of a snack—chef salad that was hardly touched and the wrappers from three Butterfinger candy bars. I rapped lightly on the door. I probably shouldn't bother Gellie, but at the moment, she seemed to be my only ally in this group.

I knocked louder. "Gellie? It's Bretta."

"Hi," she called through the door. "Can't wait to see you, but I just got out of the shower. We'll visit at dinner. Okay?"

Deflated, I agreed, then went back down the hall, arriving at the elevator just as Miriam stepped off. Her greeting, "You're just the person I wanted to see," put me on guard.

"Why is that?" I asked.

She was dressed in a jade-green linen pantsuit. The color complimented her lovely shoulder-length red hair and matched her eyes. Waving a slender hand, she said, "Bretta, you've taken too much upon yourself with this contest. You need assistance."

"I have Robbee."

Miriam's lips tipped up in a cool smile. "Robbee is a sweetheart, but let's face facts. He didn't make the competition. Becoming your assistant was the next best way of marketing his creative talent. He's here to snatch and grab whatever limelight he can weasel."

Robbee had his faults, but Miriam was hardly the person to point them out. "Robbee has stripped thorns from roses, swept floors, and carried buckets of water and bags of trash. All are mundane chores that won't get him an ounce of recognition except from me."

"Forget Robbee. Let's concentrate on the contest."

I struggled to keep my tone even. "I can assure you, Miriam, that's exactly what I'm doing."

"Delia has brought something interesting to my attention. You never refer to any kind of notes. Are you pulling all this preparation out of thin air? Chloe in the casket is different, I'll grant you that, but where do we go from there? Have you thought everything out? A competent coordinator would have a working theme. Are we making wedding, sympathy, or party designs? How can any of us prepare if we don't know what's expected of us?"

"Didn't you read my cover letter? I mailed one to *all* the contestants."

Her eyes narrowed to slits. "I've known you for years, Bretta, and I've never seen this narcissistic side. Is it your recent weight loss? Has your new look given you a different perspective? Do you have a need to exert your power over us?"

I chewed my lower lip, so I wouldn't take a bite out of her. Finally, when I had some control, I said, "If you know me so well, then you shouldn't be surprised that I'm not changing my mind."

Ignoring the elevator, I took the stairs for the short hike up to my room. As my sneakers scuffed the concrete steps I thought about Miriam's remarks and had to admit they hurt.

I wasn't being paid for this job. I had nothing to gain, but I had plenty to lose if events didn't proceed smoothly. I'd been a florist for over twenty years, and a member of this association for nearly fifteen. I had a damned good reputation for being dependable and clever, and I wasn't about to risk either on this competition. I knew I could keep the contest entertaining and fair to all the contestants—if I were left alone.

Once I was in my room, I put through a call to the

McDuffys. Thinking about them was a diversion that I needed. My plan had the desired affect. When they didn't answer, I sat on the bed and tallied the few facts in my possession.

Their notes had sounded like they were anxious to see me, so where the hell were they? Why weren't they doggedly on my tail? I wasn't that hard to find. All they had to do was follow the trail of flowers, and they'd find me.

I dug the envelope from behind the armoire and reread all the notes, searching for any scrap of information I might have overlooked.

This was the part of my personality that Carl had said would make me a good detective. Details. I thrived on them. I was a list maker—a planner. Every eventuality had to be examined and eliminated with a possible solution. What could happen? What might happen? What did happen? These were all concerns that came into play, whether I was planning a floral contest or delving into a strange situation, which seemed to accurately describe the McDuffys' vanishing act.

As I read and reread Vincent's words, I tried to make an emotional connection with what might have been going on in his mind. While it was only conjecture on my part, I knew the sorrow of losing someone you love. He'd buried his only daughter last month. The month after Carl died, I'd hardly known my name. I'd existed in a vacuum, going about my daily chores because it was my custom, not because I was motivated.

What had motivated Vincent and Mabel to come to Branson? Lois had said Vincent was a huge man. His wife had cancer. Surely it had taken an effort on both their parts to make the trip. If they'd wanted to talk to me, they could have called the flower shop.

I looked back at the letter and read the last couple of lines of the first paragraph: . . . *learned that you would be in Branson this weekend for a floral convention. We've timed our trip to coincide with this event.*

I sat up straight. Now why in the world would the McDuffys want to be here at the same time as the floral convention?

Chapter Four

🌿 An astute architect can look at a site and sketch a structure that complements its surroundings, allowing the building to draw character from its location. The restaurant on the top floor of the Terraced Plaza Hotel had been created by that kind of professional. Glass, glass, and more glass had been used to accentuate the decor. Why put framed prints on the walls when Mother Nature is the expert landscapist?

A private room had been set aside for our introductory dinner and the setup gave the impression that we were dining in someone's luxurious home. Natural wood paneling covered the walls. The carpet was the color of clouds on a stormy morning. The eight-branch candelabra, hanging above the massive table, shed its soft light on the china, silver, and three odd-looking floral bouquets. The chairs were overstuffed wingbacks, and I longed to settle myself on a plump cushion, but I hesitated in the doorway, taking stock of the occupants in the room.

Delia and Miriam were in attendance, and each was dressed in her own distinctive brand of fashion. Delia had lots of pale skin showing around scraps of red material. Miriam wore a conservative ivory suit with gold accessories that accentuated her flaming hair. Tyrone looked as suave as ever, his dinner jacket a custom fit to his lean frame. Zach's smile could melt an igloo. He leaned attentively toward Allison, who was gussied up in pink satin draped with chiffon. She looked my way, and I did a double take. The hawkish nose and deep-set eyes were familiar, but somehow—some way— Allison had tamed her customary bristly eyebrows into an orderly manner.

I was wondering if she'd used a case of Super Glue when I heard a "psst" from behind me. I looked over my shoulder and saw Alvin pushing a cloth-covered cart up the hall. The three-foot, first-place trophy rocked ever so gently as he came to a stop near me. I steadied the award and smiled at the hotel event specialist.

"Right on time," I whispered. "I hope this place has full coverage for glass breakage. When the treasurer sees the amount of money I've spent on this hunk of metal, her shrill voice might shatter a few panes."

"Let her rip, Bretta; I'd trust this glass to withstand a mighty gale."

"Gale isn't the name of this storm." I stepped to the doorway and nodded to Bernice, whose mouth was pursed as if she'd bitten into a green persimmon. Her stern gaze had settled on Effie, who'd used lavish sprays of orchids, with name tags attached, to denote each person's place at the table. "You'd think Bernice's personal income was financing this conference."

Alvin grinned. "Other than Miss Scrooge, how're things going?"

I saw Darren standing alone at the windows. "So far so good . . . I hope."

"Uh . . . Bretta, here at the hotel, we get a shipment of flowers each week for the girls to use in the restaurant and in the lobby. We don't profess to be designers, but fresh flowers lend an elegance that puts us a step above some of our competition. The staff went ahead with their work, just as they do for other dinner parties. When I realized they'd made the centerpieces for a 'florist' meeting, I thought I'd better check to see if any of you were offended by their workmanship."

I'd already noticed the arrangements and had wondered who was responsible for cramming the blossoms into the vases. There were enough flowers to make three times the bouquets. No design, no artistic quality, but I made myself smile. It was the thought that counted. "You worry too much. The flowers are fine and add a nice touch."

"Then they look okay?"

I winked. "They're fresh. Let's leave it at that."

"Thanks, Bretta. In fact, I guess I owe you a double thank you."

"Why is that?"

"Helen says those messages from the McDuffys were for you. I'm glad that was cleared up. She wasn't getting any work done for worrying."

"Have Vincent and Mabel come back to the hotel?"

"I don't know them so I couldn't tell you, but I can ask the front desk to keep an eye out for them." His round face creased with a frown. "Helen seemed to think those messages were important. Is there anything else I can do?"

"They're supposed to come to my room in the morning. So I'll just wait until then."

Alvin nodded and went on about his duties. It was time to do mine. I adjusted my purse strap over my shoulder and hitched up my panty hose. As I entered the room, pushing the cart with the trophy, a hush settled over the small group.

I smiled and quickly parked the award, then made my way to Darren. He had his back to the others, staring out the window.

"Hi," I said. "Enjoying the view?"

He continued to gaze out the window. "I never tire of it, especially at twilight—before full darkness falls and another day is gone. From here the dazzle of Branson is hidden and all you see is the natural beauty of our Missouri countryside."

If I could forget that I was nine stories in the air, the view was awe-inspiring. Haversham Hall was unlit, but the conservatory shone against the clouds. The rounded dome appeared like a full moon creeping over the horizon.

"That adds an eerie futuristic touch, doesn't it?" commented Darren before turning to survey me. "You clean up very well, Bretta. Nice dress."

I plucked the clingy black fabric nonchalantly. "This old thing? I packed the first item I came to in my closet."

He chuckled deep in his throat. "Yeah, right, and everyone in this room is filled with benevolence for me. Even as we speak, I'm being needled by a very penetrating gaze."

I glanced around and saw Delia glowering at us. " 'The blond bitch' does look a tad ticked off."

Darren grinned sheepishly. "Sorry about that scene this afternoon, but I let them get to me. After two pots of coffee and a shower, I'm ready to rise above their pettiness."

"That's good to hear. Where's Hubert?"

"He wasn't invited, and he wouldn't have come anyway. If I know him, he's ordered from room service and is watching television."

"Smart move. I'd trade places with him in a heartbeat."

I excused myself and mingled, steering clear of Miriam and

Delia, but stopping at Effie's side. She was dressed in purple, and the reflected color made her hair look like a swirl of lavender cotton candy.

When I complimented her on the place cards she'd made, she barely acknowledged my words. I asked, "Do you still have a headache?"

Effie gave an exasperated sigh. "There isn't one thing up there to ache, dear. I've lost my mind, as well as a few other things I could mention, but I won't because it would make me look like a doddering old fool."

"Which you are not."

"Thank you, dear," she said as she hurried off.

I looked across the room and noticed Bernice glaring at me while riffling through a folder. I broke eye contact before she could call me over for a discussion about the cost of a trophy that I hadn't gotten her permission to purchase. Hoping to head off a confrontation, I scurried over to Robbee.

He stood by himself but watched Chloe, following every move she made. The young woman deserved an ogling. Her miniskirt slip dress was made of a material that caught the lights and glimmered in a rainbow of colors. Of course, it wasn't the colors that had caught Robbee's eye. Her perky little nipples pressed against the fabric in an open invitation.

Robbee had removed the rawhide strip from his long hair, leaving the luxurious curls free to fall over his shoulders. Once he'd pulled his gaze off Chloe, he greeted me with a soft whistle.

"So that's what you've been hiding under your T-shirt," he said, leering at the low neckline of my dress.

"Don't be vulgar, Robbee. We've got a couple of problems—"

"—and here they come now," he finished in a whisper.

"Bretta," said Miriam, "you look nice this evening. I don't believe I've seen you in anything quite so . . . uh . . . alluring. But then, you've never had this kind of figure, have you?"

I ignored her to say, "Robbee and I were just talking about Branson. It's a lovely place with so many things to do and see. The hotel's brochure says that over six million people visit each year. I really should make the trip more often."

Robbee took my cue. "I come to Branson regularly, especially when the conservatory has a special program. Miriam, remember last year when nearly all of us in this room were at the Fleur-De-Lis Extravaganza? Every hybrid lily imaginable was on display. The blooms were incredible. I met this woman who pressed flowers into—"

"Be quiet, Robbee," said Delia. "We're not interested in your social life." She turned to me. "I think it's time you quit playing games. It's only fair that you reveal the contest—"

Tyrone's regal tone interrupted Delia. "Excuse me," he said, "but I'd like to speak with Bretta before our meal is served."

He took my arm and escorted me into the hall, but once we were alone he didn't say anything. I knew this was about the contest, so I primed myself for battle, but stubbornly waited for him to hurl the first derogatory shot.

Tyrone cleared his throat. "What I saw a moment ago didn't appear to be teamwork, Bretta. Gauging the look on Delia's face, you haven't changed your mind about revealing the contest categories."

"No, and I don't plan to."

"Your attitude isn't conducive to a working relationship with all who are involved."

I shrugged. "I can't help that."

"Can't or won't?"

This time I gave him a small smile. "Some of both, I suspect."

That wasn't the answer he'd expected. His lips thinned to a straight line. "I won't use my power as president to make you change the rules at this late date, but I *insist* on a superbly executed contest on Saturday. I want it to be unique and memorable, and my board of directors—Allison, Bernice, and Effie—tell me that you have the ability to carry it off."

This was a surprise. I knew I could count on Effie's support, but never Allison's, and Bernice was as dippy as a canoe. "What about Miriam and Delia? Will you tell them that I have the board's backing?"

Tyrone's chin came up. "I'll make that announcement, shortly."

"Miriam will be furious, and so will Delia."

"They'll get over it," was his clipped response.

I had my doubts, but we moved back into the dining room and Tyrone took his place at the head of the table. Effie flitted about the room like a purple finch, directing each person to his or her designated spot. She'd put me next to Darren, but across from Bernice.

As I pulled the chair out, I saw I was also under a cooling vent. The chilly air current was nothing compared to the frigid looks Bernice sent my way. I shivered, wishing I had a jacket to toss across my shoulders and a suit of armor to ward off Bernice's icy stare.

Zach leaned forward. "Want to trade places, Bretta? In this coat, I could use some cooler air."

I flashed him a grateful smile and circled the table taking the seat next to Robbee, which put me at the other end of the

table from Bernice. Across from me, Gellie's place was con-
spicuously empty.

"Tyrone," I said as I hung my purse over the back of my
chair. "Gellie isn't here. Shouldn't we wait for—"

"Here I am, Bretta," called a familiar voice.

Heads swiveled. Jaws dropped. I slipped weak-kneed into
my chair and gazed in awe at my old friend.

The last time I'd seen Gellie had been at Carl's funeral,
and she'd weighed a solid three hundred pounds. This new
Gellie might weigh in at one-thirty. She strolled into the
room with a proud smile that would've rivaled a searchlight
for its brilliance.

Beside me, Effie whispered, "That's the woman who nearly
smashed my car when I arrived on Wednesday. Pulled right
out in front of me when I was making a turn into the hotel
parking lot."

I nodded absently. I talked to Gellie regularly on the phone,
but not once had she even mentioned that she'd been on a diet.
The contestants had seen her last September at the semifinals,
but from their shocked expressions Gellie hadn't looked like
this.

"Ta, da!" she said, striking a cheesecake pose. "Would one
of you gallant young men hold my chair, please?"

When no one moved, I nudged Robbee, who leaped from
his chair like a startled grasshopper and hip-hopped around
the table.

Once settled, Gellie turned to Tyrone and giggled. "I'm
sorry I created such a stir, but I've waited months and months
for this occasion. Surely, you wouldn't deny me this moment
in the spotlight?"

Tyrone cleared his throat once, then twice. "Uh . . . of
course not . . . Gellie."

Emphatically, Gellie said, "No. No. Gellie was that other woman, but she's gone. She choked the life out of me. Kept me from doing and being all that I wanted. My name is Angelica, and I'm free to fly like an angel. Thank God, I'm free, and Gellie is dead."

Chapter Five

A stunned silence followed Gellie's announcement before Tyrone tapped his water glass for our attention. "This weekend . . . uh . . . promises to be . . . uh . . . one of the most . . . uh . . . exciting in the history of our organization."

I hid a grin. Even the mighty "ruler" could hem and haw with the best of them. I glanced across at Gellie, who usually shared my peculiar brand of humor. She was applying lip gloss.

Tyrone stroked his mustache and referred to a sheaf of papers in his hand. Once he'd found his place in the prepared speech, his voice was stronger, more self-assured. "The first annual Show-Me competition has brought the most talented florists in the state of Missouri to Branson. As president of this association, I welcome each of you, and wish you a hearty 'good luck' with your endeavors.

"The outcome of this contest is important, but the steps toward that final judgment are just as momentous. My name is attached to this conference, and I won't tolerate any grandstanding or embarrassing scenes. There's more to this weekend than this competition. Let me remind you that florists from all over southern Missouri are coming here to better their design techniques and implement new ideas into their businesses. Allison is chairing a number of informative work-shops. At this time we'll hear from my second-in-command."

I expected Allison to stand and salute, but she only tugged her pink-satin dress into place while favoring us with a smile. Whatever she'd used to tame her eyebrows had pooped out. Bushy hairs had sprung back to life and gave the appearance of marauding woolly worms creeping across her forehead.

"There will be four workshops," she explained, "and here are their titles. 'Long Live Fresh Flowers—processing new arrivals to your shop.' 'Advertise. Advertise. Advertise—selling your service.' "

Robbee whispered in my ear. "I've heard the speaker is from some backwater town up north but has built her business into a helluva profit-maker. I could use some pointers."

" 'Nasturtiums—edible plants and flowers,' " rambled Allison. " 'Sympathy Bouquets—buttering our bread with profit.' " She sat down to a weak round of applause.

Tyrone took over again. "The success of this conference takes a cooperative effort on everyone's part. Bernice is making sure our finances are in order. Effie is recording our decisions so future conference committees can refer to her notes."

He picked up a paper from the table and waved it. "I have here the reservation list for those attending the Haversham Hall and Conservatory tour that will take place tomorrow afternoon. Of those in this room only Bretta has signed up."

Robbee leaned close. "Suck up. Trying to find favor with the president?"

My answer was a well-placed elbow. He responded with a soft grunt.

"—see all of your names on this roster," said Tyrone. "You are the stars of this conference. I want you to mix and mingle.

Let the attendees see you and talk to you. As for myself, my door is always open. I will listen to any suggestions on how to improve the quality of this weekend."

This was it. Now Tyrone would say something about the board supporting me on keeping the categories secret. I was wrong, and gritted my teeth in frustration.

"Our industry is part of a Global Garden. Flowers are shipped from all over the world. In our daily lives, we use words such as heliconia, anthuriums, dendrobiums, bromeliads, and bougainvillea. These names sound more like pharmaceutical prescriptions than flowers."

Tyrone paused for laughter. When there was none, he continued undaunted. "In my opinion, holidays put us under more stress per situation than any other profession, other than the medical field. Our job is to provide a service with imagination and panache. We have to show our customers that while they can exist without flowers, their world is a better place because of them."

"Why is he telling us this stuff?" asked Robbee.

I shrugged.

"Global Garden refers to the ease with which we can obtain any flower at any given time. Tulips in August. Lilacs in September. Orchids. Gardenias. Somewhere in the world these flowers are available—if we're willing to pay the price. Hybridizers and growers are working relentlessly to develop something new and exciting to showcase our unique skills."

I smothered a yawn. Monarchy . . . malarkey. Effie was right about the definition of Tyrone's name. His demeanor was that of a ruler. He had a captive audience and was milking the attention for every pint.

My mind wandered. My eyes strayed to Gellie. Since she'd entered the room, I'd fought the urge to stare. It was as if my friend *had* died, and in her place was this strange woman—Angelica, who was now checking her image in the mirror of her compact. The old Gellie would have ordered a king-sized mug of coffee, laced it with four teaspoons of sugar, then dug into the rolls and butter while flashing me comical faces during Tyrone's long-winded speech.

Had my personality undergone such a drastic change when I'd shed one hundred pounds? My weight loss was enmeshed with Carl's death. When he passed away, I'd lost the taste for food. Those first twenty pounds had dropped off without any conscious effort on my part. The next eighty had been fought with a war of wills.

My desire for cheeseburgers and chocolate had come back with a vengeance, but by that time I was motivated to lose the weight. The new style of clothes I was able to wear kept me from overindulging, but I'd had some major setbacks. I was a junk-food junky and tried to steer clear of goodies that would trigger my appetite. The taste of a forbidden food sliding over my palate was enough to send me into an eating frenzy, especially if I was under pressure.

"—and now Bretta will fill us in on the design categories," finished Tyrone.

I'd only been preoccupied for a moment. Had I missed something? I whispered to Robbee, "Did he say anything about the board agreeing with me?"

"Nope."

I swung my head around to glare at Tyrone, who stared at me with exalted eloquence. Pulling in a lung full of oxygen, I slowly released it in a ladylike sigh. Nodding and smiling graciously, I came to my feet. "Thank you, Tyrone, for this opportunity. Working with you on this conference has been a valuable lesson. You are the quintessential modern-day president." I lowered my gaze on him so he wouldn't miss my implication.

Slowly I enunciated each word. "I'm the contest coordinator. I was given free rein to conduct this competition as I saw fit. I have no guidelines since this is the first such contest held by our association, but I do have experience. I have attended other floral contests. Like it or lump it, ladies and gentlemen, the categories will remain a secret."

I sank to the chair when my knees gave out. My heart was pounding so loud I was sure everyone could hear it in the silence that followed my statement. Across the table, Gellie smacked her bony hands together. "You go, Bretta. Stick to your guns. Let the chips fall where they may."

Zach cleared his throat, and eyes ricocheted from Gellie to his handsome face. I'd noticed that he sat forward in his chair as if it didn't have a back. That's probably what came of exercising come hell or high water or while at a florist convention. I was hunched over like a toad and quickly made an effort to sit up straight.

"Frankly, I don't see the hassle," said Zach. "We're professionals. We do this for a living. What difference does it make as to the categories? I'm looking forward to the challenge." He delivered a smile in my direction, then rocked back, satisfied that he'd had his say in the matter.

I nodded thank you, then saw a funny look come over his face. He gasped and leaped to his feet, turning over the chair in his haste. He acted as if he had an itch, twisting and clawing at his backside.

"Help me," he shouted. "Something is stuck in . . . my—"

He turned toward Darren, who wrapped his hand with a linen napkin. I saw him give a hard yank, then hold up a blood-smeared knife.

"Well, I'll be damned," said Darren. "How did that get in your chair?"

Zach's handsome face was etched with lines of pain. "More importantly, I want to know how it got in my ass. What fool would leave an open knife in a chair?"

"An old fool," said Effie tearfully, rising unsteadily. She wobbled around the table and took the napkin-wrapped knife from Darren. With hands trembling, she explained, "My grandnephew had it specially made for me. My old fingers can't work a regular florist knife. This one has a spring-loaded blade. When a bit of pressure is applied to the casing, the blade slides out ready for use."

Robbee said, "Holy cow! Granny's packing a switchblade. Who'd have thought it."

Effie turned to him. "I suppose you could call it that, but it isn't one of those gangster-type weapons. As you can see the blade is only three inches long, but I've . . . uh . . . honed it to a surgical sharpness."

Zach snorted. "Damned right. That blade sliced my ass like a piece of steak. I'm lucky it went through my coattail and trousers before embedding itself in my butt. If Bretta had sat here, she might've had a serious injury."

"Now, now," said Tyrone. "Let's not make this more than it is. You'd better go have that wound tended to, Zach. Ask someone at the front desk who to call."

Zach left the dining room grumbling and limping. Effie looked as if she was about to pass out. I put my arm around her shoulders and helped her into her chair. "It was an accident, Effie. He'll be fine."

"Yes, but I feel terrible. I don't understand how the knife got into that chair. I had it in the basket I brought the place cards in. I'm sure I didn't take it out."

Suddenly Delia scooted away from the table and stood up.

Effie looked her over and whispered to me. "Greek, dear. Delia means 'easily seen.' In that red outfit, she'd stop a ten-ton truck."

Delia glared accusingly around the room. "We've had our little drama, now can we get back to the important subject of this weekend? I gather that Miriam and I are the only ones that see this contest as a potential fiasco. Bretta has to be made to see that we deserve to know—"

Her speech came to a grinding halt when Gellie asked the waitress for a cup of hot water, and the young woman didn't understand the request.

"Hot water," repeated Gellie, pulling a tea bag from a zippered pouch in her purse. She glanced across the table at me and winked. "Lesser of two evils, Bretta," she said quietly.

I didn't know what Gellie meant until she said in a more normal voice, "What a wonderful idea to present a *trophy* to the winner."

I shook my head at her and tried not to laugh. Deep down inside where it counted, Gellie hadn't changed. She knew that if Delia persisted on this overworked subject, I'd be pissed, and might tell the whole group to take a hike. However, a wrangle with Bernice was wicked pleasure.

Bernice is tall, broad, and has all the finesse of an ocean liner. Cajole and flatter aren't in her vocabulary. She speaks her mind, has the last say, and takes pleasure in leaving demoralized bodies in her wake. I just didn't plan on being one. Before she spoke, I turned to her, knowing what was coming. She didn't disappoint.

"Where is the bill for that trophy? How much did it cost?"

I named a figure that caused her to slump against the table. Her speechlessness lasted for a breath, but when she opened her mouth, I was ahead of her. "I haven't gone over my allotted budget, Bernice. With so many donated items, I'm justified in spending the money. The trip to Hawaii is wonderful, but I want to hand the winner something special when he or she succeeds."

"You should have told me. Keeping hidden expenditures from the treasurer is a sure way of getting things out of kilter. I'm responsible for every cent, and I intend for these books to show a profit." She glanced at Tyrone before peering suspiciously at me. "Which reminds me. Where is the bill for the shipment that was delivered about an hour ago?"

Frowning, I asked, "What shipment? The contest flowers will arrive in the morning."

"When I was in the basement a Federal Express man brought a huge box. There was no bill of lading. No invoice. Nothing."

I wondered what she was doing in the basement. "Perhaps it's another donation."

"From California? What wholesaler from out west is going to donate flowers for a contest in Missouri?"

"Maybe it's a direct shipment from the grower. I won't know until I check my notes."

Delia had sat down, but now she leaned forward. Her tone was sarcastic. "You mean you really have something written down? There are plans? There are notes? There is a list of categories?"

"Yes, Delia. I've worked damned hard on this contest."

"So you say, but we haven't seen any proof."

"Now, ladies," said Tyrone, "I will not tolerate this bickering. Adverse undercurrents will be sensed by the attendees and put a damper on the festivities."

"This contest could be fun for everyone," I said. "If *everyone* will back off."

Miriam surveyed me coolly. "Bretta won't change her mind, and we're using our energy arguing a lost cause. We'll have to prepare for the competition in another way." She looked across the table at Darren and flashed him a smile. "How about sharing some of your wonderful design techniques? I'm curious how you can come up with one fantastic piece of work after another and another."

Before Darren could speak, a trio of tray-bearing waitresses came into the room. The aroma of food turned my stomach, but more upsetting was the company I'd have to keep while eating. I pleaded a headache and left the dining room.

The headache hadn't been a lie, but I didn't want to shut myself in my room. I stepped to the door of the main dining room, but it was crowded, not a single empty table in sight. The bar was open, but I wasn't a drinker or I'd have hopped on a stool and knocked back a couple of margaritas.

I bet Zach could use a stout potion to dull the pain of his wounded posterior and pride. It wouldn't help his macho image to be seen gimping around the hotel, favoring his butt. I was sorry it had happened—sorry for him and for Effie, but I was glad Zach had traded chairs with me. In this flimsy skirt and panty hose that knife would have scored a deeper hit, and I'd have been out of commission.

In the hall I looked around wondering where to go, and what to do? The new shipment of flowers popped into my mind. When in doubt, do what comes naturally: work. A long flight from California meant the flowers needed water.

The hall was congested with people waiting for a table. I sidestepped several, murmured "excuse me" a couple of times, then hurried past the elevators to the stairwell that would take me to the corner of the basement nearest the storage rooms designated for our contest.

I had opened the stairwell door when a hand touched my bare arm. The contact was warm but surprising. Startled, I turned to find Bailey smiling at me.

"You look upset," he said, nodding to the stairs. "Shortcut to your room?"

"Nope. Basement."

He grinned. "Really feeling low, huh?"

That's the kind of comeback Carl used to make, and I smiled at the memory. But my lip action froze when I met Bailey's warm gaze.

Abruptly I said, "An unexpected shipment of flowers has arrived, and someone needs to cut the stems and put them in warm water. I decided I might as well do the job since I'm not feeling very sociable." I tacked this last on hoping he'd get my drift.

"I'd like to see these flowers," he said, taking my elbow and urging me through the stairwell doorway. The door clunked shut behind us.

I smothered a resigned sigh. Short of being rude to him, I didn't see how to get rid of him. We were silent as we went down the first flight of steps. The aroma of his aftershave lotion was pleasant but thought-provoking. I'd know that scent anywhere. Carl had worn Old Spice every day of his life.

Bailey clomped behind me, not saying a word. Finally, I said, "Besides being an avid gardener and butterfly enthusiast, what do you do?"

"I'm a deejay for a radio station outside of St. Louis. I play golden oldies for my audience."

That was my favorite music, but I'd never have pegged Bailey as a rock and roller. I glanced over my shoulder at the easy way he wore his suit. The navy jacket was neatly buttoned.

His burgundy tie hung straight, the knot tied with precision. "I'd have guessed you were an IRS man, banker, accountant— a suit and tie kind of profession."

"Really? I'm most comfortable in jeans and sneakers."

I stopped to massage my left foot where a blister was forming. "Me, too. These heels weren't made to traipse down nine flights of stairs." I looked at his feet. Spit and polish penny loafers without the pennies. In place of the copper coins, Bailey had substituted dimes. An interesting piece of trivia, and when I had a free moment, I might speculate on what it meant.

"I assume we're taking this route because you were in too much of a rush to wait for the elevators?" asked Bailey.

I slipped my shoe back on and started down the steps again. "I hate heights and those glass-fronted elevators are too exposed for my taste."

"Oh, so you have a case of acrophobia. My second wife was claustrophobic. Could barely tolerate an open closet door. She'd toss my shirts at the hangers and seem amazed when none draped themselves obligingly around the wire frames. Of course, my third wife wasn't much better. Her problem was allergies—vacuum cleaners, washing machines, ironing boards, and dishwashers. You name it. If it involved moving off the couch, she became incapacitated."

I couldn't keep from sounding flabbergasted. "You've been married three times?"

"Guilty as charged. I'm not proud of my mistakes, but I'm not accepting all the blame. It takes two to make a relationship. My first wife was a paragon. When she passed away, I should have been content with memories of a good marriage."

"What happened to her?"

"Car crash. Slick roads. It's been five years, but the pain is still there."

"Yeah. My husband died twenty-two months ago."

Bailey whistled softly. "Tough time. I remember it well. You don't fit in. Still feel married, but no spouse. No spouse, but it's difficult going out with anyone."

Finally someone who understood. Lois was forever pushing me to date and telling me to "get back in the scheme of things." I looked over my shoulder at Bailey. "That's right. I've tried dating, but I feel as if I'm cheating on Carl."

"I thought wife number two would fill a void in my life. Instead of solving my problem, she created more than I wanted to handle."

I hurried on down the stairs. That's what I feared. Carl and I'd been in sync with few minor discords. Behind me, Bailey continued talking. "I divorced her and swore off any serious relationships. I dated a few times, but mostly I sat home. Then I met my third wife and fell for her like a randy teenager. She was beautiful, even laughed at my jokes."

"This was the wife allergic to housework? You could have hired a maid if she was perfect in other areas."

"Not perfect by a long shot. Did I mention that she gained forty pounds in the six months we were married?"

"Oh?" I kept my tone neutral. "Do you have an aversion to heavy women?"

"Women who don't care about their looks irritate me. Fat women, in particular, annoy the hell out of me. They blame genetics, sluggish metabolism, underactive thyroid, or some such medical problem, when all they need to do is shut their mouths and get up off their wide behinds."

His insensitive words hurt. Right then and there, I should

have set Bailey straight that overeating has many contributing factors and rarely is laziness among them. I should have told him that I'd once been overweight, but I'd never spent my time lounging around the house. Perhaps I'd eaten the wrong foods, but I wasn't a slacker. However, those explanations were too personal to make to a man I didn't know. Instead I navigated the last three flights of stairs in silence.

At the basement door, I turned to Bailey. "I can take it from here, Mr. Monroe. As I said before, I'm not feeling social this evening."

Bailey's brown eyes widened. "That's a cool dismissal. We were doing fine when we left the ninth floor. In fact, between the sixth and fourth, I thought we shared a common understanding of what it was like to be left without our spouse. What happened, Bretta? What did I say that annoyed you?"

I didn't bother answering. I opened the door and went down the corridor toward the storage room. To my irritation, Bailey followed. If he couldn't take a hint, then I'd have to spell it out. I wasn't interested in his company, and if he knew the truth—that I'd once been a fatty—he wouldn't be interested in mine.

I faced him and said, "You're right about one thing. It does take two to make a relationship. You might want to take a closer look at your own actions before you place the blame for the failure of your marriages."

Instead of taking offense, Bailey flashed me a winning smile and grasped my arm. But before he spoke, his breast pocket rang. He frowned and took out a cell phone. It was shiny chrome, tiny, and compact—just the way he liked his women, I was sure.

"Monroe," he said. "Yeah. Yeah."

I tried to pull away, but Bailey's fingers tightened. "Wait," he said to me. "Not you," he rumbled into the phone. "Go ahead."

This man was testing the limits of my patience. I jerked my arm. His eyebrows drew down into a frown. "Can't say," he murmured. "Can't say." He cupped the phone closer to his lips. "Bodies?"

I froze, but cocked an ear.

Chapter Six

Hearing the word "bodies," and being the widow of a law officer, my mind instantly went to homicide. Carl had taken calls like this a number of times when we'd been married. Thinking back, it seemed that most of the requests to report for duty had come at night. I'd lie in bed and watch him dress to go out to investigate a scene that would keep him absorbed to the point that neither of us could rest until the case was solved.

In view of where I was, and whom I was with, it was a ridiculous assumption, but I didn't think about that. As soon as Bailey had slipped the phone back in his pocket, I asked, "Whose bodies? What happened?"

"Bodies?" he repeated, frowning. "Oh. A couple of butterflies were caught in a net. In their struggle to get free, they thrashed themselves to death." He touched his jacket pocket. "The president of our organization asked me to help him mount the bodies on a poster to insure this kind of torture doesn't happen again."

"That's the silliest thing—"

Bailey's tone was chilly. "I have my hobby, and I take it very seriously. Capturing butterflies that are burdened with eggs is against our club policy. Those butterflies are dead because a couple of members wanted a closer look at the markings on the wings." He dropped my arm. "You'll have to excuse me. I have work to do."

I stared after him as he hurried down the corridor and through the basement doorway. I didn't buy that bit about the butterflies for a second. Something was going on, and my next best guess was shapely bodies. Bailey had been on the make in the lobby and later in the bar and the elevator. It sounded to me as if he'd gotten a call from a friend who'd arranged a hot date.

Out loud, I said, "Mount the bodies," and was shocked at the inappropriate way my body responded.

"Carl, I wish you were here," I said, calling on the best defense I had against these stimulating thoughts. But this time there was no answering voice. I hoped it was because my mind was crowded with other things, and not because Carl had slipped away. As time went on would his voice dwindle until I never heard it again?

I couldn't abide pursuing this, so I let my guard down and thoughts of Bailey crept in. It was interesting that we had several things in common—the loss of a spouse was an emotional bond that not everyone could understand. When Bailey had mentioned his first wife, I'd detected a deep sense of loss, but to marry two more times seemed irresponsible, if he was only lonely. He had said he was an avid gardener, so he liked flowers, which was a redeeming quality to this florist. But he couldn't abide fat women.

I sighed and meandered down the basement corridor. For the preparation of the contest, I'd been assigned two rooms with a connecting door. One room contained a walk-in cooler, while the other had easy access to water and trash pickup.

The hotel forbid handing out storeroom keys to guests. This had been the deciding factor in making the categories secret. Since I couldn't stop the contestants from snooping, I had to have some way to keep their work spontaneous during the competition.

To my way of thinking that's the only way to judge creative talent. If they were prepared with the knowledge of the flowers, the containers, and the categories, they could map out their strategy. How would natural ability come into play?

I opened the door to the storage area where I'd directed the hotel staff to put any deliveries for our convention. Alvin had just cut the twine from around a large box.

He straightened when he saw me. "Hi. I thought you were eating dinner."

"Don't you ever rest?" I asked.

"Not when there's so much going on at the hotel. Weekends give me that 'red-eye flight' look." He nodded to the box. "One of the girls told me a shipment had arrived. I've learned it pays to get the flower stems into water as soon as possible. Since you were busy, I thought I'd help out."

"Thanks, but I need the therapy. I might complain about being overworked, but when I'm upset, I always head for the buds and blooms."

"I go to the lake. There's nothing like sitting in a boat with the wind in your face, the sun on your back, and the smell of a fresh-caught bass."

"Nice picture you've painted, but it's dark outside. With both Taneycomo and Table Rock Lake nearby, I know there's plenty of water, but no available boat. As for the fish—" I sighed. "I see it fried to a crispy golden brown and surrounded by potatoes and coleslaw."

"Sounds like you're hungry."

"My own fault. I left the dining room as the waitresses were bringing in the meal. Eating while peeved makes for a bad case of indigestion. I've got enough problems without getting a stomachache."

"Are you still peeved?"

I grinned. "No. I've mellowed out."

"Do you like hot chicken wings and French-fried onion rings?"

"I love them." If I was really mellow, I'd have said, "No thanks, I steer clear of those high-caloric snacks." However, I kept my mouth shut and watched Alvin go to a wall phone and poke two numbers. I could have stopped him when he gave the order and added two glasses of iced tea, but my lips refused to say the words.

When he'd hung up, and it was too late, I said, "That's nice of you, but not necessary. I won't waste away without one meal."

"I haven't eaten either, and we have to keep up our strength. The weekend is just starting."

"Tell me about it. Once it's over, I can go home and settle into my same old rut." I shook my head at him. "How do you do it? Conference after conference, followed by crisis after crisis. Or is my conference the only one that's a pain in the ... uh ... hibiscus?"

"That must be florist jargon because I'm not familiar with that particular body part."

I chuckled. "I could have expressed myself in more vivid terms, a habit for which I'm noted, but I was trying to be polite."

"Relax, Bretta, it'll work out. Everyone comes here to get

away from that 'same old rut' as you so aptly put it. If the beds are comfortable, the service is efficient, and the food is delicious, who's going to complain?"

"I hope you're right." I studied him thoughtfully. "How did you get into this business?"

Alvin leaned against the wall and talked as I filled a couple of buckets with warm water. "I started a career in the Peace Corps. Now I cater to the 'lush' and 'gush' of our society." He made a face. "I've dealt with both ends of the spectrum— famine and deprivation and gluttony and abundance. Overseas, I literally got sick from all the deplorable sights. I had to come home to recuperate."

Alvin gave me a sad look. "It's a fact that children are starving all over the world. I couldn't make myself go back overseas, so three times a year, I produce a benefit performance at the open-air theater that's part of the Haversham Hall estate. All the proceeds go to an orphanage in Somalia."

"Alvin, I had no idea. That's admirable and very—"

"I'm not doing anything fantastic. Tell me how you became a florist?"

I was in the middle of my tale when the food arrived. While talking, I'd filled several buckets and was ready to pry off the lid from the box of flowers. Alvin suggested we eat before we cut stems. My stomach growled agreement.

The waiter had put the food on a small table after we'd cleared it. As Alvin and I sat down, I studied him, looking at him in a new light. His smile was shy; his eyes twinkled good-naturedly.

"I'm impressed with what you're doing for those kids overseas. Most people talk about it, feel bad, but don't do anything. If you'll send me information about the next benefit, I'll see to it that you have coverage in my hometown paper." I raised my iced-tea glass in a toast. "Good luck and congratulations."

Alvin clicked his glass to mine. "Thanks, Bretta. It's a deal." He took a slurp, then wiped his upper lip with a napkin. "Now let's talk about this floral conference. What's got you so upset that you'd walk out on that—what did you call it?—introductory dinner?"

I picked up a section of a chicken wing and took a bite. Alvin would be impartial and from what I'd discovered he was a good listener, but did I really want to talk about the contest?

I chewed and after swallowing reached a decision. "Let's just forget it. We'll eat this great food, and then cut the flower stems. Afterward, I'll toddle off to bed, and tomorrow morning, I'll wake up with a clearer head and a brighter outlook."

"Sounds good." He dipped an onion ring into the puddle of catsup on his plate. "You know what this snack calls for?" he asked, casting me a conspiratorial glance.

My mouth was full. "Hmm?"

"A piece of blackberry cobbler, or there's coconut cream or chocolate pie. Take your pick."

"I can't eat all that before I go to bed. I won't sleep a—" My willpower fled at his offer of my favorite dessert. "Did you say coconut cream?"

We were visiting, having a good time, when the door opened and Gellie stuck her head in. Seeing me, she demanded, "How many storage rooms are there in this place? I must have opened twenty doors before I heard laughter. I knew it was you. There's no mistaking that cackle."

She came into the room, eyeing the food and licking her lips. When she saw Alvin, she smiled. "A party? I hope I'm invited." She unzipped her purse. "I don't suppose I could get a cup of hot water?"

Purse. I whipped around looking for mine. I searched under the table, on the back of my chair, then stopped as memory surfaced. I'd left it hanging on the back of my chair upstairs in the private dining room.

"Sit here, Gellie. I'm leaving." I explained about my purse. "But first I have to put these flowers in water."

"Is that the shipment Bernice was ranting about?" asked Gellie. When I nodded, she continued, "Bernice has a bad case of tunnel vision. No matter what the subject, she focuses all her attention on it until she drives everyone around her bananas. When she won the association's bid for treasurer, I knew she'd be hell-on-wheels with this conference."

I pulled the lid off the flower box. "As long as we stay within our budget, what difference should it make to Bernice?"

Gellie chuckled dryly. "Bretta, you really ought to attend more floral meetings so you'll be privy to all the gossip. Bernice has a thing for Tyrone. After he told her that he expected the association's bank balance to show a marked increase after the conference, she went into high gear, pinching pennies and doling dollars like a tightwad, hoping to please our esteemed president."

Alvin took the cardboard lid from me and leaned it against the wall. "I'll do these flowers, Bretta, if you want to get your purse."

"First let's see what came from California," I said, pushing away the plastic packing material. I rocked back on my heels. "I'm not impressed. I was expecting exotic blossoms, not this stuff."

I pulled a woody branch out of the box. The leaves were dark green and shiny with touches of bronze on the new shoots at the tips. I held it up for Gellie to see. "What is this? Do you recognize it?"

"No, but like Tyrone said, growers are coming up with new products every day. At least it's dramatic and has a sturdy stem."

I nudged the cardboard container with my foot. The mailing label directed the shipment to me here at the hotel. "There isn't an invoice, so I assume we aren't being charged. That should make Bernice happy."

"I don't mind putting these greens in water," said Alvin. "They have a nice, clean smell."

"I'll help him," offered Gellie. She shooed me away. "Go get your purse, but let's meet for breakfast. I want to talk to you."

And I wanted to talk to her. Had Effie been mistaken when she said it was Gellie who had pulled out in front of her at the hotel? What was Gellie doing in Branson yesterday, when she'd phoned me and said she couldn't arrive until today because she'd had car trouble? If she had come to Branson earlier, why keep it a secret? I also wanted to quiz her about Darren. He harbored some pretty intense feelings toward her, and I wondered what had happened to cause them.

The McDuffys were coming to my room at seven. How long would it take to talk with them? Ten minutes? Half an hour would be better. Gellie agreed to meet me in the hotel café at seven-thirty.

In the hall I decided I was too tired to climb the stairs. I found an elevator marked SERVICE and pushed the button. I wasn't sure where this ride would deposit me, but figured I could find my way. The bell soon dinged, and the doors slid open.

On the balcony I took a minute to get my bearings. The dining room was across the abyss, so I started around the perimeter. As I walked, I glanced down to the fifth tier of rooms and located my door—seventh from the end. I wished I were in bed and asleep. My stomach was full and—

I stopped and squinted. Was my door open? Silently I counted from the corner room—one, two, three, four, five, six—it *was* my room and there was a light on.

I hung over the railing for a better look. Reality took a swing at my stomach, and I nearly showered those teeny-tiny people in the lobby with chicken chunks. I flung myself away from the chasm and galloped around the balcony and down the four flights of stairs to the fifth floor.

Like a shadow with respiratory problems, I wheezed along the corridor that led to my room. Maybe it was a cleaning lady, I thought to myself as I stopped to catch my breath. I eased the door open and peeked inside. From this angle I couldn't see anything.

I stepped farther into the room and saw my open purse on the floor. On the bed was the key card, its plastic surface covered with something that looked like blood. I stepped closer, seeing droplets on the beige carpet. I thought the room was empty until I heard muffled sobs coming from the bathroom.

I nudged that door open a few inches, and my heart nearly stopped. Bloody fingerprints rimed the sink. A bloodstained towel was wadded on the floor. I pushed the door open wider and saw Delia leaning against the wall. Her eyes were closed, her skin the color of ashes.

"Delia, what happened?"

Her eyes opened slowly as if she were awakening from a bad dream. She licked her lips and mumbled something. I didn't catch what it was, and repeated, "Delia? What happened? Where did all this blood come from?"

"Me," she said. "I could have bled to death, and it would've been your fault."

Chapter Seven

I took a step toward Delia. She came out of her daze with a shriek. "Stop! Don't come any closer. As soon as my head clears, I'm out of here."

"Why are you in my room?"

"I took your purse from the dining room, and I used the key to get in here. I had to know if you're taking this contest seriously. You surely have a list of the categories written down somewhere. This contest is important to me, but nothing warrants booby-trapping your door."

"Booby-trapping? What kind of booby trap?"

Delia didn't answer right away. She loosened the towel from her hand. With the palm held toward me, I saw blood trickle from a four-inch cut that crossed three of her fingers. Tears welled up in her eyes. "I'm out of the contest. I can't work with my hand like this."

"Why did you say my door was booby-trapped?"

"Razor blade taped to the door handle." She gulped and shuddered. "It was a reprehensible act. What if a maid had come by? What if a child had gotten mixed up on which room was his?"

A razor blade?

I spun on my heel, headed for the door. I jerked it wide

open and stared at the handle. Nothing. I looked at Delia, who'd followed me. "There isn't anything here."

"What?" She leaned around me so she could see for herself. "It was there." She held up her wounded hand. "I have the proof."

I touched the metal lever and felt a tacky residue that might have come from a piece of tape. "Something was here, but it's gone now." I looked Delia straight in the eye. "I didn't do this. I wouldn't do anything so horrendous."

"If you didn't put it there, then who did?"

"I haven't a clue, but if it's someone's idea of a practical joke, that person is in for some serious trouble."

I went to the phone and called the front desk, explaining that an assault had occurred on the fifth floor. In three minutes flat the night manager was on the scene. Delia told her tale. The young man listened, looked at the handle, made a few notes, and assured us that he'd alert his supervisor. He offered to arrange medical attention for Delia's hand.

Before they left, I took Delia aside. "I'm sorry this happened, but I didn't have anything to do with it."

"I probably know that, but right now I'm in pain and too upset to think about it."

She turned to go, but I touched her on the arm. "Please don't tell anyone about this. If that person is to be caught, it might be best if he isn't alerted."

Delia didn't agree or disagree. She lifted a shoulder, and then cradling her injured hand, followed the manager to the elevators.

I looked up and down the hall. There were low-watt wall lights to guide guests to their rooms, but the bulbs wouldn't have been bright enough to show a sliver of stainless steel. The thought of someone taping a razor blade to the handle was as Delia had said—reprehensible.

Somehow the use of that blade was as shocking as an outright attack. It ranked right up there with the sadistic pleasure of putting laxatives in brownies and thumbtacks on the seats of chairs. I gulped. Or a knife wedged in a cushion so the blade would slide from its casing and puncture an intended victim.

My door. My room. My name tag. My chair. Knife. Razor blade.

A shudder wracked my body. A gun to my head would have aroused the same reaction, except a gun carried an obvious threat. A razor blade was stock household supplies. My God, I shaved my legs with Carl's old safety razor. I'd handled the pieces of steel since I was twelve years old, and treated them with respect because they sliced tender flesh.

I searched the balcony, wondering if the person responsible was lurking about to see if his sick joke had brought results. No one was in sight, but that didn't mean I wasn't being watched. I went into my room and locked the door, putting the security chain on. For several minutes I stared around me, wondering if I was being unduly suspicious, but I couldn't shake the feeling that I'd been the target. But why? Outside of irritating the contestants by not revealing the categories, I'd been minding my own business.

Before going to bed, I packed all the paraphernalia back into my loaded handbag. I cleaned the bathroom and took a hot shower to help me sleep, but a good night's rest was in short supply. By six-thirty the next morning, I was dressed in jeans, a rose-pink sweater, and sneakers. The McDuffys' envelope waited on the bed.

As I paced, I eyed it and worried about a number of things. After my breakfast with Gellie, I faced a tough day. First order would be processing the flowers—stripping foliage from the stems that would be below the waterline in the buckets. Once the flowers had revived from their journey, they had to be separated into five groups since Delia was leaving the contest.

This afternoon was the tour of Haversham Hall and Conservatory. I was looking forward to visiting the palatial grounds and glass greenhouse conservatory. Back home I was rejuvenating my own gardens, and I hoped to get some ideas I could whittle down to accommodate my newly acquired acreage.

I checked the time again. It was five after seven. I unlocked my door and stepped into the hall. I saw no one, but something was lying on the carpet. It wasn't until I touched it that I thought of fingerprints. It was an empty cartridge of what had once held Schick razor blades. I turned the case over and over in my hand. Where were the rest of the blades?

I crept across the balcony and peeked over the edge to the lobby below. A few people milled about, but even from this height I could tell none fit the description Lois had given me of the McDuffys. I directed my attention to the café. Gellie was already at one of the tables.

I turned the handle to go into my room and felt the sticky reminder of what had happened last night. I looked across the balcony to the opposite tier of rooms. What kind of sadistic mind would think of razor blades as a warning—a deterrent—a threat to keep me from doing what?

I should check on Delia, but I didn't want to tie up the line in case the McDuffys were trying to reach me. I dropped the cartridge in my purse, then stared at the McDuffys' envelope. Where were they? It was almost a quarter after seven.

I went to the phone, but my call to the McDuffys went

unanswered. Now what was I supposed to do? I was tempted to open the envelope, but Gellie was waiting, and a shipment of flowers would arrive shortly. I grabbed up my purse and wedged the envelope into a side pocket.

The calves of my legs ached from all the stairs I'd climbed yesterday. This morning I took the elevator to the lobby. As the cage descended, I kept my gaze on my clenched hands. When the bell dinged and the door opened to the lobby, I lifted my head and locked eyes with Bailey.

He was dressed in the same suit pants he'd had on last night. The jacket was draped over his arm, and the burgundy tie trailed untidily out of a pocket. Whisker stubble darkened his jawline. His eyes were red-rimmed.

I stepped out of the elevator, and Bailey gave me a weary smile. "You're up early," he said. "Got a fun-filled day of sightseeing planned? I never asked when you got into Branson?"

"Wednesday morning, but no sightseeing. This is a working holiday for me." I nodded to him. "Looks like you had a busy night. Mounting those butterfly bodies must have been exhausting."

He shot me a sharp glance. "How about breakfast? Afterward, we can take a drive up into the hills and see the view from—"

I looked past Bailey and saw Gellie waving from the café. "Sorry," I said, and was surprised to find that I meant it. "I'm meeting a friend for breakfast, and I'm keeping her waiting."

I crossed the lobby and sat down at Gellie's table, but my attention was on the ascending glass box. Bailey stood in the corner, staring at me. As the elevator rose higher and higher, his facial features blurred. But in my mind I continued to see his smile and hear his voice.

Gellie touched my arm. "I had the waiter bring you coffee,

Bretta. I've also ordered a fruit plate." She nudged the colorful platter closer. "Dig in."

Food was the last thing I wanted with my stomach in turmoil. How could a man I'd barely met cause me such confusion? With a deceptive calmness, I popped a strawberry into my mouth. As I chewed, I forced myself to concentrate on Gellie.

She wore jeans, a denim shirt, and just the right touch of makeup. "You look great," I said. "How'd you do it? How'd you lose so much weight so quickly?"

"It didn't seem fast to me. Dropping one hundred and sixty pounds takes time. At the semifinals I'd lost eighty, but I disguised my loss under those old tent dresses I used to wear. I wanted all the weight off before this Branson trip so I'd get the reaction I got last night." She chuckled. "It was worth all the pain I've gone through."

"Pain?"

Gellie lowered her voice and leaned forward. "I don't tell everyone, Bretta, but I had my stomach stapled. Doctors only do the procedure when a person is morbidly obese." She shook her head dismally. "It makes me sick saying the words and knowing they apply to me. My stomach is only a fraction of its original size."

I remembered the Butterfinger candy bar wrappers that I'd seen on the tray outside her room. "So you can eat anything and your weight remains stable?"

"No. I wish that were true." She picked up a bunch of grapes and plucked one. Instead of putting it in her mouth, she rolled it between her thumb and index finger. "My body has changed, but I still have the mind of a fat woman. I can't leave the sweets alone. I don't gorge like I used to, but I can eat candy, milk shakes, and brownies in small doses. Lately I've gotten into the habit of drinking a milk shake rather than eating a healthy meal."

Her voice choked. "The result is I'm gaining weight. I've put on eight pounds in the last week." A lone tear rolled down her cheek. "What am I going to do?"

I stared at Gellie, and Bailey's hurtful words slipped over my lips. "Shut your mouth and get up off your wide behind."

Gellie blinked in surprise.

I gave a rueful grin. "Sorry, but that's what someone said to me not long ago. I took offense, but maybe he was right. I've been on every fad diet that was ever invented. I've drunk grapefruit juice before each meal. I've cut the fat. I've cut the sugar. I've added more carbohydrates. I've counted calories on one diet, and fat grams on another until the arithmetic made me grab a calculator. I can hardly look at a plate of shredded lettuce with tuna piled on top."

"I know. Statistics show that dieters regain nearly all their lost weight in the second year. How do you do it, Bretta? I'm afraid I'm going to become another morbidly obese statistic."

"I try to eat right, but I still fall off the wagon and resort to old habits. There's no magic cure."

Suddenly Gellie waved her hands as if clearing the air of a foul smell. "Enough of this. I'm tired of talking about it. Tell me how you've been? Are you keeping busy at the shop? How's Lois?"

We talked like old times, covered a lot of ground, but I still had another topic that I hesitated bringing up—Effie's notion that Gellie had lied about her arrival time in Branson. Rather than confront Gellie outright, I tried to be subtle.

"I've missed you," I said. "I'm glad you're here. I was worried when you had car trouble. I could have come and got you."

"Thanks. Tow charges are terrible, but I couldn't leave my car on Highway 65."

I licked my lips uneasily. "Sixty-five? I thought you had trouble on Interstate 44."

Smooth as custard, Gellie said, "Forty-four—Sixty-five, they both come together in Springfield. My car conked out, but it's fixed and I'm here."

Her tone implied that the discussion was over, but I couldn't let it drop. "Effie says she saw you on Wednesday. In fact she says you almost hit her car when you pulled out of the hotel parking lot."

"Nope. Wasn't me. Effie's sweet, but her eyesight isn't what it used to be."

I didn't agree. From what I'd observed, Effie could see as well as any of us. I took a breath, and I called Gellie on it.

Gellie tapped her fingers impatiently. "All right, Bretta, I arrived in Branson a day earlier than I led you to believe. I had an appointment. Last year when I was in Branson, I was approached with an idea, but I wasn't interested. After giving it some thought, I decided I wanted more information. So I arrived early."

I also figured Gellie wanted to get settled in her room so she could make her entrance before any of us saw her. "What's going on with you and Darren?" This question curdled the custard.

Gellie's chin shot up. "What's he been saying about me?"

"Not much, but I got the impression that the two of you are on the outs."

"More than outs, Bretta, he's furious with me and has been since the semifinals. I challenged him on a design." She studied me. "Surely you've heard the story?"

When I shook my head, she leaned forward. "I told you that you should get out more and attend these florist meetings. Miriam discovered that Darren had come to the semifinals with prefabricated glamellia blossoms. You know how long it takes to wire the florets of a gladiolus around each other until the blooms are the size of a saucer? Darren had three exquisite ones ready and waiting to use in his bride's bouquet. None of the rest of us had that advantage. Miriam wouldn't do anything, but I called Darren on it to the judges."

"And he got mad?"

"Are you kidding? He was livid. But the judges agreed with me."

"He still placed in the finals."

"Sure he did. He's a talented man. Look how he's invited all over the world to conduct design symposiums. He knows every trick of our trade."

She leaned sidewise in her chair to look around me. "You have another visitor headed this way, and I have things to do."

I whipped around, thinking it might be Vincent McDuffy. It was only Allison. "Just what I need this morning," I said.

Gellie nimbly rose to her feet. She smiled down at me, but her eyes swam in tears. "I can't gain this weight back, Bretta. I love being this size. I'm only fifty. I still have a chance for a life."

She moved off to the elevators, and Allison plopped down in the vacated chair. Nodding to Gellie's slender back, Allison said, "I have to admire her for losing all that fat. She used to be as big as a house."

"What a compliment. I hope you won't mind if I *don't* pass it on."

Allison waved her hand. "Whatever. I'm here to give you a bit of advice. I don't know how you're going to pick the winner of the contest, but you'd better not have any input on deciding the outcome."

"I don't." Wearily I put my elbow on the table and propped up my chin. "The judges will be the audience. Ballot boxes will be placed by each design at the end of the contest, and everyone will vote on his favorite from each class."

"Not bad. Judged by their peers. Makes for audience participation, which is always good. Who's doing the tabulation?" She looked at me from under woolly eyebrows. "Not you and Robbee, I hope?"

"No. I've asked Alvin to assemble some hotel employees for that chore."

"Good. Good. Sounds like it'll work and should be fun."

"Should be, but it isn't. So far nothing about this trip is fun." I studied Allison. "By the way, do you know Vincent and Mabel McDuffy?"

Allison shrugged. "They own a farm next to my husband's brother. When Mabel was in the hospital, I sent her a bouquet." She snorted. "Fat lot of good it did. When Stephanie died, your shop got the family's flower order."

I was aware of Allison's cheap business tactics. I knew for a fact that she toured all of River City's funeral homes so she could read the sympathy cards and discover the names of her competitors' customers. She'd joined the River City Country Club to hobnob with the cream of our society, and she rotated her attendance among three different churches, angling for a job on their flower committees. However, sending a bouquet to someone in the hospital, with the hope of acquiring future business, had to be an all-time low, even for her.

"Why are you interested in the McDuffys?" Allison asked suspiciously. "Has Mabel taken a turn for the worse?"

"Not that I know, but that's an idea." I pushed back my chair and headed for the nearest telephone.

Chapter Eight

My calls to hospitals within a fifty-mile radius of Branson netted me nothing on the McDuffys. I was at a loss as to what I should do next. "Do nothing" was my first thought, but I had their envelope in my purse. According to the instructions in the note, I had their permission to open the package and "assess" the contents. But I wasn't going to do that in the middle of the lobby.

I moved on to the conference meeting room where Effie's arrival at the door coincided with mine. "Hello, dear," she greeted me. "I couldn't sleep after last night's mishap, so I thought I'd look in on the bouquets. I asked that the room temperature be kept as low as possible, but it never hurts to double-check." She glanced past me and smiled. "There goes that nice man who escorted me to the dining room last night."

I turned and saw Bailey crossing the lobby. He'd cleaned up since our last encounter. His thick hair had the appearance of having been freshly washed, and he'd changed into a different suit.

"I think he's interested in you, dear. He asked me several questions."

I swung my attention back to the older woman. "What kind of questions?"

"He asked how our conference is going, and if you handle details well." She patted my hand. "I assured him you take each of your duties very seriously."

"And that's all he wanted to know? How well I handle details?"

"Well no, dear. He asked about your husband. That's why I think he's interested. He wanted to make sure you were single. I told him Carl had passed away two years ago. That's when he commented that you're a fine-looking woman."

She quirked an eyebrow. "I don't think anyone should base a relationship on a physical attraction, but that's what tempts most men. I told him you had the willpower of a saint. That you'd shed pounds and pounds."

"And you say this conversation took place last night *before* the introductory dinner?"

At her nod, I looked back at Bailey, but he was headed out the front doors. "He just arrived and now he's leaving. Wonder where he's going?" I answered my own question. "Only one way to find out. I'll follow him."

"Really, dear, isn't that a bit forward? Of course, your generation—"

I left her in midsentence. Mr. Bailey Monroe had shown entirely too much interest in me. Watching me in the lobby. Offering me a stool next to him in the bar. Catching my elevator and initiating a conversation. Making the nine-flight trek with me to the basement. But the real kicker was discovering that he'd known I'd once been heavy, but he'd still made that nasty comment about fat women. What was his game?

I made a beeline for the front door, but came to a halt when I saw Bailey outside the entrance, buying the morning newspaper from a vending machine. While he fumbled for the correct change, I zeroed in on my car, which was clear across the parking lot. If he was leaving, I was out of luck if I wanted to keep a discreet tab on him.

Effie huffed up next to me. Breathlessly, she put a shaky hand to her heart. "My, but that was quite . . . a sprint. I haven't moved like that since a stray cat tried . . . to eat my canary. Stopped the feline before a feather . . . had been ruffled, but the close call made the bird . . . neurotic for the rest of his life."

"My car might as well be on the moon for all the good it's going to do me. If I cross the lot at that angle, Bailey's sure to see me."

"Bailey?" asked Effie. "Then you know him?"

"I know he doesn't like fat women."

"I see. You're out to prove a point. My car is over there, dear. We can take it."

I followed the direction of her finger and saw three cars near a row of lilac bushes that had been planted as a screen between the newly constructed miniature golf course and the parking lot. I started to nod, then her last words registered. We?

Gently, I discouraged her. "It might be best if you stayed here, but if you'll trust me with your car, I'll be back in about—"

Effie's lavender curls danced like wisteria in a spring breeze. "Sorry, but it's a package deal, and you'd better decide. Your gentleman is headed for that black and silver Dodge truck."

I craned my neck and saw she was right. Bailey was on the move. "Let's go, Effie, but I'll drive."

"Of course, dear. I have my keys ready."

They jingled annoyingly as we slipped out the door. The shuttle buses were lined up for the morning tour of Haver-

sham Hall and offered us cover. Alvin leaned in the open door
of the first bus, sharing a laugh with the driver. I gave them a
casual wave as I zipped along the line of lilac bushes headed
for the green Pontiac. Effie, however, stopped next to a black
Volkswagen Rabbit convertible and proceeded to unlock the
driver's door.

"This is it," she said proudly.

Numbly, I walked to the car and looked inside. There was
only one word for it—small. No, I sighed, as I folded myself
behind the steering wheel. Make those two words—really small.
The pedals were the size of S.O.S scouring pads. My rear felt
like it was sitting on the ground, and how in the world was I
going to move my legs to operate this tin can?

"I don't think this is going to work, Effie. I haven't driven
a stick shift in twenty years, and my feet are too big for the
pedals."

Effie peered like a feisty squirrel over the car's canvas top.
"Mr. Bailey is backing out of his parking spot. Here let me
adjust the seat. Your legs are much longer than mine." She
reached down and flipped a lever, and I found myself staring
up at the headliner. "Oops. Wrong one. Sit up straight."

I struggled into an upright position just as she pushed
another lever and the seat slammed into place, whacking me
across the shoulders. Before I could catch my breath, she'd
pulled another mechanism making the bucket seat slide back-
ward. I wiggled my feet, which were about ten inches from
the pedals.

"You have to cooperate, dear. I can't do everything. Now
adjust your seat and let's go." She rounded the bumper to the
passenger side and got in. "Lucky for us they're unloading
supplies for the miniature golf course, and your Mr. Bailey had

to make a detour around to the service exit." She pointed. "See? There he goes."

I started the car and heard the engine hum like a sewing machine. I pressed on the clutch and put the car in reverse, touching the gas pedal tentatively. We lurched out of the parking spot.

"Have you played miniature golf, dear?" asked Effie, looking out the side glass.

I suspected she was trying not to laugh. "Many times," I answered, applying the brake. I pressed on the clutch, put the gearshift into first, and we hopped across the asphalt. "Rabbit, indeed," I muttered, grinding the gears as I searched for second.

"From my hotel window I can see this golf course. 'The Wonders of Missouri' is a charming idea for showcasing famous landmarks and distinguished Missourians." Effie chuckled softly. "Though, I have to question what Mark Twain and George Washington Carver would have thought at having their likenesses decorating a theme park."

I followed a narrow lane behind the hotel and saw the service exit. Synchronizing the clutch and the gears, we careened around the corner headed east on Highway 76. Sunlight glinted off of Bailey's truck as it took the first in a series of curves. I gave Effie's car more gas and shifted into third and finally fourth gear.

"Is it difficult to play?" asked Effie.

I had to think back to what she'd been talking about. "Miniature golf?"

"Yes, dear. Imagine batting the ball and making a field goal under the watchful eye of Mark Twain."

"Putt the ball, Effie, and if you sink the ball in the cup in the right number of strokes, you get par. High scores in other sports. Low scores in golf."

"I don't understand, dear, but it doesn't matter. At my age, it's too late to learn." Tears filled her voice. "Besides, I'd probably forget what you told me."

"You can forget one thing, Effie," I said, glancing at her. "Stop worrying about Zach and that knife. You didn't have anything to do with what happened."

I'd been diverted for only a few seconds, but it was enough to misjudge the sharp curve we were entering. I quickly applied the brakes, and Effie pitched forward.

"You're speeding, dear. While I can understand your impatience, arriving in one piece is preferable, especially since we're in *my* car."

When I eased off the accelerator, Effie said, "Life is so fast paced. Look at your friend, Angelica, losing all that weight in such a short time. I didn't recognize the woman when she pulled out in front of me on Wednesday. I'd met her at the semifinals, but I never put the two women together as being the same."

We'd entered Branson with two cars and a van between Bailey and us. Effie kept talking, but I shut her out, concentrating on keeping the black and silver truck in sight. We traveled down Highway 76, passed one music theater after another until we crossed Highway 65 and entered historic downtown Branson. Bailey turned left, then right. I dropped back a block so as not to draw his attention.

As we drove along the quiet streets, I got the impression of any small town in Mid America—no flashing neon signs, gaudy paint, or oversized billboards. This was the sane side of town, where people worry over family budgets, children attend school, and as I spied the sign for a local funeral home, where people die and others mourn their passing.

I'd scarcely completed that thought when Bailey pulled into the funeral home's parking lot. I stopped on the street and hunched down, but Bailey didn't look around. He climbed out of his truck and entered the back of the building.

Effie leaned forward so she could see around me. "Eternal Rest Chapel," she said, reading the sign. "I hope your Mr. Bailey didn't receive bad news."

"He's not *my* Mr. Bailey, Effie. Did you happen to notice the name of this street?"

"Pine Tree Lane, and not a pine tree in sight."

I put the car into gear and slowly pulled away from the curb. I drove around the block and spotted a service station. The Rabbit's gas tank was full, but I needed a place to stop and think. I parked the car away from the pumps and stared off into space. For once, Effie was silent, and I took advantage of the moment.

For Carl, detecting had been a matter of using his mind over his brawn. He abhorred violence of all kinds. Truth be known, he hadn't been able to kill a mouse. But he'd solved a number of Spencer County crimes, and not once had he used his bulk to bring a criminal to justice. Outthinking, outsmarting, and outmaneuvering had been his credos. He'd contended that God had given us a brain, and we'd do well to use it.

I put my gray cells to work, and the first word to pop up was bodies. I'd thought Bailey's explanation had been lame concerning the butterflies, but it wasn't my business to challenge him. It still wasn't, and yet— Why was he showing such an interest in me?

I'd like to think it was my captivating personality, but he'd been watching me in the lobby before I'd opened my mouth to him. Like Effie said, it might be a physical attraction, but my figure, which represented a personal triumph, was hardly a traffic stopper.

Why had he gone to a local funeral home? He'd bought the morning newspaper at the hotel. Maybe I'd better check out that newspaper, too.

I started to unzip my handbag to dig for money but saw the McDuffys' envelope in the side pocket. No one had seen the McDuffys. They hadn't come to my room at seven nor had they made any further attempt to contact me since ten o'clock Wednesday evening.

"I'm going to use the rest room, dear," said Effie. "I'll be right back."

I nodded absently, taking the envelope from my purse. Now I didn't hesitate. I peeled off the tape, upended the envelope, and watched three items tumble into my lap. One was a note bearing my name.

Mrs. Carl Solomon:

In this crazy world we live in, change seems to be manda-tory. I wish our Steffie had been the exception. A year ago this past June, when she returned from a three-day trip to Branson, she had changed, and now she's dead.

Mabel and I are looking for the person who led our daughter astray. We don't have much information to share with you, but Steffie played this music cassette continually after her return from Branson. She'd sit in her room, sip tea, listen to the music, and wait impatiently for the mail to arrive.

Mabel wanted you to see what a pretty woman our Steffie used to be. I've enclosed a snapshot that was taken before she

deteriorated. Look into her eyes, Mrs. Solomon, and you'll
see a kind and trusting soul. Someone took advantage of her,
and we want that person punished.

> *Mabel and Vincent McDuffy*
> *Spencer County, Missouri*

The photograph had landed facedown against my jeans, but I reached for the cassette instead. It was a Kenny Loggins single release titled "Whenever I Call You 'Friend.'" I was familiar with the song, could even hum a few bars, but the lyrics eluded me.

I turned the photograph over, and for the time being, ignored the figure, taking in only the background. To the right of Stephanie was the corner of a white-porch railing, to her left a flower garden. She looked directly into the camera. I looked directly at her and took a shaky breath.

When I was about her age, this could have been a picture of me. Not the hair or the eyes or the facial features, but the triple chins, the thick waistline, and the fat thighs. I did as her father had asked and looked into Stephanie's eyes. A veil of love had distorted Vincent's vision if all he saw was his daughter's kind and trusting soul. What I saw was an overwhelming depression that stooped her shoulders and kept her smile from being genuine. This was the image of a very unhappy young woman. It was as if I'd lived in her body. I knew her pain. I'd heard the hurtful remarks made by people who thought they were being helpful, and others who didn't care how their comments cut.

I stared at the photograph. Stephanie and I had never met, but in a sense, we were well acquainted. Her eyes pierced mine with a look I'd carried most of my life.

"Poor girl," I murmured. We were kindred spirits. I thought the McDuffys had asked for my help because of what

Carl had told them. But perhaps, the couple had hoped I'd understand their daughter's anguish.

But what could I do? Lois had said she thought Stephanie had died from a heart attack. Had her weight been a contributing factor to her heart problems? What kind of change had the McDuffys meant? How had Stephanie been led astray?

From my purse, I took the original note that had been taped to the outside of the envelope and reread it. Once again I was caught by their reference to my solving two murders. Had Mabel and Vincent found the person who'd led their daughter astray? My heart lurched. Had that person not wanted to be discovered?

Bodies? Funeral home?

The car door opened, and I jumped in surprise.

"—bathroom was a disgrace," said Effie as she settled herself in the seat. "I always feel as if I've been exposed to a dreaded disease when I use public rest rooms."

"Effie, I want you to call that funeral home—"

"The Eternal Rest Chapel, dear?"

"That's right. I want you to ask when you can deliver the sympathy bouquets for the McDuffys' service."

"Where shall I make this call?"

I nodded to the booth outside the gas station. "We'll do it from there, okay? I'll be right beside you, listening to what is said."

Effie studied me pensively. "I won't ask why now, but later, I'd like an explanation."

As I got out of the car, I murmured, "So would I, Effie, so would I."

I bought a newspaper from the rack and tucked it under my arm. While I looked up the funeral home number, I rehearsed Effie on the dos and don'ts of subterfuge. "Carl used to say that the big boys—"

"Big boys, dear?"

"The professionally trained investigators. Carl used to say that they like to answer a question with a question. Since we don't come close to their expertise, I think we'll do best to say as little as possible. Try to sound casual. Keep your wits about you."

"Good gracious, it's not as if I'm calling the Pentagon for classified information. I phone my local funeral home often, asking about different services. I'm sure the people at the Eternal Rest Chapel are used to this kind of inquiry."

I took a deep breath to settle my nerves. Effie was right. It was a simple inquiry, except I was afraid of the answer. What if the call Bailey had gotten had been about *human* bodies? But why would *he* get a call?

My stomach muscles were tied in knots as I picked up the phone and poked in the numbers for the funeral home. At the first ring, I handed the receiver to Effie, who was as calm and composed as I was frazzled.

I put my head close to hers and heard a man say, "Eternal Rest Chapel. This is Anthony."

"Anthony," said Effie, "when can we deliver the sympathy bouquets for the McDuffy service?"

"McDuffy?" He gasped. "How did you— I . . . uh . . . I . . ."

Suddenly Bailey's unmistakable voice boomed in our ears. "Anthony didn't catch your name, but I understand you're inquiring about a service. How may I help?"

Effie opened her mouth, but I pressed her arm and shook my head.

"Hello," said Bailey. "Who's calling? I know you're on the line. Speak up! Why are you asking about the McDuffys?"

I took the phone out of Effie's hand and quietly hung it up. "Let's get out of here."

This time I had Effie slide behind the wheel, while I slumped in the passenger seat. "Just drive, Effie, but steer clear of the funeral home, and we might as well stay away from the hotel, too, at least for a little while. I'd rather not run into Bailey just now."

"Why do you think your Mr. Bailey came on the line? Does he have a connection with the funeral home?"

"I don't know."

"Why didn't that nice-sounding Anthony answer my question? And who is this McDuffy?"

"Please, Effie, I need to think. If you'll drive for a while, then I'll try to answer your questions. Okay?"

She nodded and turned on the ignition. Like a pro, she shifted gears, and we shot out of the service station lot into a stream of traffic. Seeing that she was more than capable at the wheel, I leaned back and mulled over the situation.

I still didn't know who Bailey Monroe was, but one thing was for certain, he hadn't liked the question about the McDuffys. A tiny smile teased my lips. I'd outmaneuvered him. I'd learned that the McDuffys were of interest to him, otherwise why had he come on the line? His voice had been cold with authority. His tone let me know that he was accustomed to having his questions answered, and he expected results.

I sank farther into the seat and opened the local newspaper to the front page. Near the bottom was a news brief that made my skin prickle.

COUPLE FOUND DEAD AT BOTTOM OF RAVINE.

(Names being withheld pending notice to family.)

I stared out the window at the trees that were a kaleidoscope of earth tones, and felt physically ill to my stomach. I could be wrong that the dead couple was the McDuffys, but I didn't think so. They had been in plain sight at the hotel for four days, and then had suddenly disappeared.

I knew so little about them and their daughter Stephanie. What I needed were solid facts. I sat up straight, coming out of my daze. "Where are we, Effie?"

"You said drive, so I'm driving. We're on Highway 65 headed north. I'd rather travel the open road than creep along in Branson's stop-and-go traffic. I'd planned to intrude on your thoughts before we got to Springfield."

A highway mileage sign loomed ahead. I skimmed over the first three towns, honing in on River City. We were a little over an hour away from home, but the scheme I was hatching didn't include entering the city limits. What I wanted was outside of town. In the "outer reaches" of Spencer County.

Chapter Nine

✿   Wearily, I closed my eyes. I was tired after my sleepless night, and the breeze coming through the open car window was soothing. I'd stalled Effie's questions for the time being, so she'd turned on the radio and was humming happily.

When we were closer to our destination, I planned to stop and call Robbee. By now the contest flowers would have arrived, and he'd be wondering where I was. I also needed a Spencer County telephone book, so I could look up the McDuffys' address. I wanted to dig up some personal information on the McDuffy family, and what better place to start than in their neighborhood.

I fell asleep with the words "dig up" in my subconscious. I dreamed I was in a flower garden, and Bailey was Adam to my Eve. His fig leaf covered his essentials. My "leaf" was a shovel. If I lowered it to scoop the soil, I exposed the stretch marks that were like battle scars that told the tale of how misshapen my body had been. But if I didn't use that shovel, truth and justice would be buried forever. I urged Bailey to go away so I could uncover the facts, but he only smiled and shook his head.

Frustration woke me, but I found I was eager to get on with my plan. I looked out the window and saw familiar landmarks. "Once we crest this hill, Effie, you'll see a McDonald's. Pull in, and I'll buy you a snack."

"I need their rest room worse, dear. My water pill is working overtime."

I touched her lightly on the arm. "You've been a good sport about this. After we finish our business inside, I'll try to explain what's going on."

While Effie was in the john, I found the McDuffys' address in the local phone directory. After I'd made a note of the road name and number, I placed a call to the Terraced Plaza Hotel. I didn't want to personally speak with Robbee, so I left an ambiguous message. Since I was already connected to the hotel, and in light of the news brief in the paper, I asked if Helen was available. She came on the line all abuzz with information.

"You won't believe what's happened?" she whispered into the receiver.

It was on the tip of my tongue to say, "The McDuffys have been found," but I stopped myself. "Tell me," was all I said.

"A DO NOT DISTURB sign has been hung on Mr. and Mrs. McDuffys' door. I've asked around, but no one knows who put it there or when." She took a deep breath. "But the big news is that the police were here. They towed the McDuffys' car out of the hotel parking lot."

"Did they give a reason as to why they were taking it?"

"I asked that same question, but the officer in charge told me it wasn't any of my business."

"I guess we'll have to wait for an answer."

"I don't like it. I've got this creepy feeling that something bad has happened."

I wanted to tell Helen that her intuition was grounded in

reality, but I kept my mouth shut. I'd learned from Carl that an ongoing investigation could be jeopardized by a careless remark. For some reason, the McDuffys' deaths were being concealed. Before I said something I might regret, I told Helen I'd talk with her when I got back to the hotel, then ended our conversation.

Effie wasn't happy that the McDuffys had lived on a gravel road. She drove her little black car as if the tires were made of marshmallows, and each time a rock pinged against the undercarriage, she winced as if she'd felt the blow.

"How much farther, dear?" she asked.

"That last mailbox had 981 painted on the side. We want 1004, so it'll probably be a few more miles. Houses are spaced far apart here on County Line Road. This is cattle country. Most of these farms are anywhere from three to six hundred acres."

I smothered a sigh. Idle chitchat, when time was slipping by. I wanted to ask Effie to step on it, but she'd been a real trooper. She'd listened carefully to everything I'd told her about the McDuffys. I'd read her both notes and the three messages. I'd shown her Stephanie's picture, but her car didn't have a tape deck, and she'd never heard of Kenny Loggins.

I looked over my shoulder at the mailbox we'd just passed. "We're getting closer. The next box will be the one right before the McDuffys'. Why don't you turn in there, and we'll have a chat with their neighbor?"

"I'm still not sure why we made this trip, dear. What kind of information are we seeking?"

"Anything is better than what I have."

"What kind of questions will you ask?"

"I don't know."

She glanced at me. "And you say you've done this kind of thing before?"

"I used to help Carl with his investigations. Since his death, I've delved into a couple of matters on my own."

"And that's what the McDuffys are referring to in their note to you?"

"Yes." I admitted it reluctantly.

"You don't sound very enthused, dear. If you made an investigation, you must have been interested in discovering the outcome."

"I do care, Effie, but it's more than that. Since Carl's death, I've gotten involved in some rather dangerous situations. When someone needs my help, I can't seem to stop from getting involved."

"Then don't try. Bloom where you're planted, dear. Why analyze and criticize your abilities? Perhaps you have a God-given talent for this kind of thing. Your husband must have been proud of you or he wouldn't have expressed his pride to the McDuffys. And it sounds to me as if they needed someone who cares. Grief affects everyone differently. You help others, and the McDuffys wanted your expertise to ease the pain from having lost their daughter."

"It's too late to ease their pain. I'm sure they're dead."

"From what you've told me you could be right."

"Now more than ever, I want to find out what's going on, but I have more questions than I have answers."

"But isn't that part of the thrill? The unearthing of the facts? If everything were laid out for you, where would be the satisfaction?"

I smiled weakly at the little woman. "Bloom where I'm planted, huh? Even if it feels as if my roots are sometimes struggling through rock?"

Effie chuckled pleasantly. "Adversity builds character, dear," she said, applying the brake. "This mailbox is 1003, which should be the one before the McDuffys'. Shall I turn in here?"

I saw the name "Thorpe" on the mailbox and nodded. She drove down a tree-lined lane. The white clapboard house, when it came into view, looked as if it had been designed and constructed by a ten-year-old. Judging the multiple rooflines, I'd guess four different additions had been made to the original structure. The house sat on a knoll, and the land gently sloped away to pastures with a lake in the valley. White geese swam lazily on the glassy surface, while cows grazed their fill on the spring grass that fringed the water's edge.

It was a classic picture of peace and tranquillity, and Effie sighed with appreciation as she parked the car. "If I lived here I'd hang a swing from that maple tree and never grow tired of the view."

The door at the back of the house opened, and a woman struggled out with a loaded laundry basket. She wore a pair of faded blue jeans and a green-checkered shirt. Her face was broad, her hair a mop of brown curls. I hopped from the car and strode across the grass toward her, dodging the bicycles, tricycles, and wagons that littered the yard. She had seen me, acknowledged me with a nod, but with the cumbersome load, had kept up a fast pace to an already crowded clothesline.

"You've been busy this morning," I said in greeting.

"Every morning," she grumbled, dropping the basket to the ground with a solid plop. "We have eight boys, and the laundry is unreal. I've never been able to decide if we're the cleanest bunch in the county or the dirtiest."

"Eight boys? Wow. Talk about being outnumbered by the male population."

She chuckled. "We also have Harry, the dog, and Bob, the cat."

"How old are they?"

She raised an eyebrow as she grabbed the corner of a purple-and-lavender-striped sheet. "Harry and Bob?"

I laughed, taking hold of the sheet and helping her pin it to the line. "And you keep a sense of humor, too. No, I was thinking of your boys."

In a singsong tone, she recited, "Fifteen, twelve, eleven, nine, the twins are seven, five, and two. Wally, Billy, Tommy, Timmy, Jerry and Terry, Tony, and Patrick. That's my tribe."

I pulled a matching pillowcase from the basket. "I saw the name on the mailbox. You're Allison's sister-in-law?"

"That's right. I'm Lavelle Thorpe, and you're Bretta Solomon." She ducked her head, but I saw her smile. "I've heard a lot about you, but I discount most of what Allison says. I've read about you in the *River City Daily* newspaper, and my neighbors, Vincent and Mabel McDuffy, have spoken of you." A frown creased her forehead. "I thought you were at that floral thing in Branson? In fact, Vincent and Mabel were looking forward to meeting you."

"I had to make a fast trip home, but I'm going back to Branson. I received messages from the McDuffys, but our paths haven't crossed yet. If you have time, I'd like to ask you a few questions?"

"About what?"

"Like I said, I've gotten messages from the McDuffys but they didn't tell me exactly what they wanted. I wondered if you knew."

"No, but you could have knocked me over with a feather when Vincent came by and told us he and Mabel were going to Branson. Since he retired from trucking cattle to market, they rarely set foot off their property, totally content to be with each other."

Lavelle smiled sadly. "Stephanie's death was a blow to them, but they had each other. When Mabel goes, I don't know what Vincent will do. He has no other family, and he cherishes Mabel."

She sighed. "I don't know what I'll do either. They're good neighbors—good people but a bit overly cautious. It took them two weeks to plan this trip. A few days before they left, Vincent was by and mentioned that he thought he ought to have the electricity shut off at his house. He was afraid there might be a short or something while they were gone. I reminded him that Missouri weather is unpredictable, and we could get a cold spell. With no heat in the house, the water pipes might freeze. He was even going to sell their chickens, but I told him my older boys would look after the flock."

I felt a chill against the nape of my neck. Had Vincent gone to Branson knowing that he and Mabel would be in danger? Had he suspected that they might not be coming home?

Lavelle was still talking. "—assured him that I'd keep an eye on everything." A note of envy crept into her voice. "Imagine just packing up and taking off. No dishes to do. No dirty clothes to contend with." She gave a pair of jeans a brisk shake. "But I'd wash clothes for the rest of my life if it meant I could keep each and every one of my boys healthy."

"You're thinking about their daughter, Stephanie?"

She nodded. "What a waste of a kind and talented woman. I felt sorry for her. She didn't have a social life. All she had were her pictures."

"Pictures? She was a photographer?"

"No, more like an artist, but not with paints or colored pencils. She used dried flowers that she pressed, then glued to mats before framing them." Lavelle glanced at Effie's car. "If you have a minute, I'll go get the one she gave me?"

I assured her I had plenty of time, and she went off to the house. I continued to hang up the clothes, a relaxing task I hadn't done in a long, long time. When the back door opened, I turned, expecting to see Lavelle, but the gaping doorway discharged a mad rush of boys headed directly for Effie and her little car.

The older woman's jaws dropped, and her eyes widened with astonishment. In a flash the kids had circled her car, fingering the cloth top, touching the side mirrors, leaning in the open window to get a glimpse of the minuscule interior. Seeing that she had an appreciative audience for her pride and joy, Effie climbed out to point like a proud parent to all her baby's sterling qualities.

"Cars, trains, bikes, trikes, and wagons," said Lavelle, crossing the yard. "Sometimes, I think it might be worth getting pregnant again, just so I'd have the chance to sew a bit of lace to a pink dress or stumble over a doll in the dark instead of a Hot Wheels race car." She sighed. "But with my batting average, having a girl is pretty slim odds."

She watched her brood gloomily. "There's no school today. Teachers needed a day off." She rolled her eyes and held out the picture. "Here's an example of Steffie's work. I keep it in our bedroom so nothing will happen to it. I tell those boys no basketballs in the house, but sometimes, it's like speaking into a vacuum."

I took the eight-by-ten frame and turned it so the sunlight didn't glare off the glass. What I saw made me catch my breath. I'd expected a piece of amateur artwork, with dried flowers scattered in a still-life motif—a technique Stephanie might have learned at an artsy-craftsy seminar. This went beyond a novice's work. Stephanie had re-created the painter Claude Monet's style of colors, texture, and shapes in the landscape. I was looking at an exciting replica of one of his "Water Lilies" paintings. Instead of oils, Stephanie had used flower petals that exploded with vibrant color on her canvas. There were no vigorous brush strokes, but an overlaying of delicately preserved natural components—twigs, seeds, leaves, hulls, husks, and petals. The results were incredible.

"Oh, my," I said. "I've never seen anything like this."

"Stephanie loved flowers and color. Those blue larkspur petals came from my own garden. So did the poppy seeds that form the dark background at the back of the pool. The delicate pinks are from my mother's roses. The mossy green is blades of grass from our own yard. Steffie didn't simply create works of art. She put emotion and personality into each picture."

Lavelle held out her hand, and I passed the picture back to her. Using her shirttail, she wiped the glass. "I treasure this, but not only for its beauty, but because Steffie was my friend."

"Friend," I repeated, thinking of the music cassette that had been in the envelope. "Did she have a particular singer she admired? Perhaps she saw a show while she was in Branson?"

"She didn't go to any of the theaters. From what I gathered, all she was interested in was a lily show that was being held at some conservatory. I teased her that she was visiting what is advertised as the 'Country Music Capital of the World,' but she said she wanted to spend time smelling the flowers."

Lavelle stopped and stared off into space. Softly, she said, "I saw her the day after she got back from Branson. My, but that young woman was flying higher than a kite because she'd met a young man on the conservatory tour. They'd shared a common interest in flowers, and she'd showed him a couple of her pictures. He'd promised to call her, and she was over the moon with hopes and dreams."

Lavelle shook her head sadly. "Stephanie described this 'fabulous' being, and if her glowing account was accurate, I can't see how he was truly interested in her." Her voice deepened with emotion. "I loved Stephanie. She would sit, and I mean *sit*, with the boys so I could have an hour or two away. She could hardly walk because of her bulk. No. That young man wasn't interested in her romantically, but I'm sure he saw bucks when he looked at her artwork. That was the attraction, at least on his part."

"What was his name?"

"Couldn't tell you. She might have said, in fact, I'm sure she did, but I don't remember."

"What about this 'glowing account'? Do you remember that?"

Lavelle grinned sheepishly. "Not really. I'm afraid I didn't take her seriously. She talked about growing more flowers, and changing for a man she'd just met."

"And did she change?"

"She got sick. She couldn't sleep, and she fought for every breath she took. I figured her heart was giving out on her, but she wouldn't go to a doctor. She said he'd only relate every symptom to her weight."

Tears filled Lavelle's eyes. "I feel bad because those last months of Steffie's life, I didn't find the time to visit her. I knew she wasn't well, but the boys had a round of chicken pox. Billy broke his foot playing basketball. The little one was teething. I had my hands full here at home. Her casket was closed, so I never got to see her again."

Lavelle dashed a hand across her eyes. "I'm sorry, but

Steffie was only twenty-seven." She thought a minute. "I remember her telling me that this man she met in Branson was in his thirties." Triumphantly, she added, "And he had long hair tied in a ponytail."

I could see Lavelle wanted me to be pleased at her recollection, but my heart had sunk to my toes. Robbee wore his long hair in a ponytail. Robbee had been to a hybrid-lily show. Last night before the introductory dinner, he'd said, "I met this woman who presses flowers—" Delia had cut him off before he'd finished speaking, but maybe, he'd said all that was necessary.

Chapter Ten

🌸 "You look sick, dear," said Effie as I climbed in next to her. "The boys wanted to see a topless car, so I lowered the roof. It might be a good idea if I kept it that way. Fresh air is a wonderful restorative."

I answered absently. "That's fine."

She opened the glove compartment and pulled out a lavender scarf, which she tied over her hair. "I love the freedom this convertible gives me, but if I don't cover my head, I'll look like Medusa by the time we get back to Branson."

She started the car and merrily tooted the horn at the group watching us depart. "What a family," she said as we left the house behind. "I don't envy that woman, yet her children were precious and well mannered, once I told them I'd cut their fingers off if they abused my car." She snickered. "Their eyes grew as big around as teacups, especially the little tikes. Of course, I was only joking, but it never hurts to get your bluff in right from the start."

"Hmm."

"Which way?" asked Effie.

We were back out at the road. "Since we're this close, I want to see the McDuffys' house. We can pull down the lane, take a look, and then head on back to Branson." I checked my watch and sighed. "It'll be after one before we get to the hotel."

Effie put the car through its paces so effortlessly that I hardly felt her change gears. After a quarter mile, she murmured, "Here we are, dear." She turned the steering wheel to the right.

"Stop. Stop!" I shouted.

Effie slammed on the brakes. "What's wrong?"

I pointed to the side of the house where a navy and gold Spencer County patrol car was parked. It was none other than Sheriff Sidney Hancock's mode of transportation.

"Back up, Effie, and when you get on the road pull over."

Once she had the car situated, I peered uneasily through the trees. About three hundred feet from the road, the house wasn't shabby, but it wasn't pretentious by any means. It was a comfortable old farmhouse with a nice porch, and well-maintained outbuildings. The flower garden that had been in the picture of Stephanie was a neglected tangle of weeds. No khaki uniforms had rushed out the door ready to give hot pursuit, so I hoped we hadn't been seen.

"A sheriff's car wouldn't be here unless events were serious," said Effie quietly.

We couldn't be overheard, yet I answered in a hushed tone. "I'd say you're right. And what could be more serious than murder, unless it's a double homicide? Vincent has been described as huge. Mabel has cancer, and I've been told she's as thin as a wafer. Helen said the police have towed away their car. Someone took them to the place where they died, and the police are making sure that the McDuffys' own car wasn't used for that purpose."

"What are we going to do now?"

"Everything I've said is speculation. I wish I could talk to

Sid in a rational manner, but that's out of the question. If he suspected I was anywhere near here, he'd bluster and blaze and threaten to have me arrested."

My gaze lighted on the FRESH EGGS FOR SALE sign nailed to a fence post. I chewed my lower lip for a minute, then asked, "Effie, how do you feel about doing a bit of amateur detecting?"

"It would be purely amateur, dear. What do you have in mind?"

"Drive up to the house and buy a dozen eggs."

"I don't eat eggs. My cholesterol has a tendency to be—" A light dawned in her china-blue eyes. "Aha. Subterfuge, again. I understand. And where will you be, while I'm playing Miss Marple?"

I told her I'd wait down the road in a patch of shade. Even as I spoke, I was having second thoughts, but Effie was chomping at the bit, ready to take on anyone and everything.

"I never dreamed when I came to Branson that I'd have such an adventure. I thought I'd be attending those boring workshops of Allison's, and here I am on a quest for the truth."

"Just remember, Effie, you can't let anyone know about this . . . uh . . . quest. Subtlety will get you more information than a flat-out question. I can tell you right now, Sid won't volunteer a thing. You'll have to be smooth, and maybe even devious if we're to learn anything."

As I got out of the car, she mouthed the words "smooth and devious" as if she were chanting a mantra. I stifled a sigh. This wasn't going to work. I must have had a brain cramp, but there was nothing for it than to let Effie try. She was high on adrenaline, and I knew what that was like. I just hoped at her age, she didn't stroke out.

My eyes widened at this horrible thought. I turned back to the car. "I've changed my mind, Effie."

"Too late, dear. Wish me luck." She wiggled knobby fingers and took off, leaving me in a cloud of dust.

The next fifteen minutes passed with all the anxiety of a trip to the dentist. I paced the gravel road, wondering for the fortieth time, "What was I thinking?" Sweet little Effie didn't stand a chance matching wits with Spencer County's obnoxious, opinionated, crotchety sheriff.

I heard a shout from the direction of the McDuffys' house and spun on my heel. Sid was on the front porch, waving something at Effie. Was he threatening her?

I hunkered in the weeds and watched as Sid came down the steps. I glanced at Effie. She hadn't moved. Had fear immobilized her? I looked back at Sid. What was in his hand?

I squinted and nearly wilted with relief. He was holding an egg carton.

"That was fun, and I got an added bonus of a dozen eggs," said Effie after she'd picked me up.

I'd put off cross-examining her until we were out of the immediate vicinity. If I'd known Sid was so close by when we'd stopped at the Thorpes', I'd probably have turned around and headed back the way we'd come. I thought about that for half a second, then shook my head. No, I wouldn't. This was the kind of thing that made me feel alive, that I was worth something to someone.

Once we were headed in the direction of Springfield and points beyond, I turned eagerly to Effie. "So what did the sheriff say? What did you say? What did you use as your cover?"

"Cover?" murmured Effie, confused by my Nancy Drew vernacular. She peered over the windshield at the sky. "Are you talking about my car's top?"

I quickly hid a smile. "No, Effie, I just wondered what kind of excuse you gave Sid for stopping and asking questions?"

She lifted a stooped shoulder. "I simply said I was worried about Vincent and Mabel. I hadn't heard from them and was out of fresh farm eggs and thought I'd stop by to see how they were."

This time my lips spread into a wide grin. "Well, that's original. The important thing is did it work? Did you get any information?"

"I'm not sure. Sheriff Hancock told me I'd have to find another source for my eggs. He also said that in a few days, the McDuffys would be kissing Bernard's porcelain table. I don't think I misunderstood the sheriff, but what in the world did he mean?"

I made a face. "That's an example of Sid's tasteless wit. In some of the older funeral homes the embalming tables are made of porcelain. Bernard Delaney is one of River City's funeral directors."

Frustrated, I slapped my thighs, making them sting. "Damnit! Damnit! It's not fair, Effie. I feel as if I've let them down. I never got the chance to tell them that I'd help. That I'd try to do something."

"I'm sure they knew you'd carry on."

"Carry on? How? I don't know what to do next. Bailey has answers, but I don't think he'll give anything over to me."

"I've been thinking, dear. The name 'Bailey' has an Old French origin that means bailiff—man in charge. Perhaps your Mr. Bailey is a police officer."

I looked at Effie as if she'd sprouted horns and a forked tail. "Wow, Effie, you're good. That would make perfect sense." Ruefully, I muttered, "But why the hell didn't I think of it?"

"You're too close, dear. Besides, I think when Mr. Bailey is around, your guard comes up because you like him and you don't want to."

Well, that was a crock, but I didn't tell Effie that. Instead, I dwelled on the more pertinent information. "If the call he took last night was about the discovery of the McDuffys' bodies, does that mean he was here at the hotel for another reason?"

"I don't know."

"I have to find out *why* the McDuffys were killed."

"Not *who* killed them?"

"From past experience I've learned that when you delve for the motive, the guilty party will slither out of hiding. Stephanie died last month, yet the McDuffys waited until I was in Branson before they made the trip or even contacted me." Thinking of Robbee, I added, "Or was it the floral convention and its attendees that were important?"

"I'm not understanding, dear. If I'm to help, you'll have to be more specific."

Uneasily I studied Effie. The rush of air from the convertible had whipped color into her cheeks. Her eyes were bright with interest. For someone who's seventy-one years old, she's as naive as a child and just about as defenseless. Poking and prodding didn't always reveal the killer, or at least maybe not right away, but it does make him nervous, and very, very dangerous.

Effie's skin was as fragile as a piece of crepe paper. A razor blade would do serious damage to her aged flesh. I shuddered at the thought of Effie pitted against the sadistic mind that had resorted to using a razor blade as a weapon. Effie was as kind and trusting as they come. Once we were in Branson, I'd gently but firmly ease her out of the picture.

At the hotel, I encouraged Effie to go to her room and relax. I went to the basement, where I found Robbee surrounded by a sea of cut flowers. Immediately, he let me know that my prolonged absence had irritated him.

"I got your message," he said, flipping his ponytail over his shoulder. "Such as it was. Couldn't your sightseeing trip have been postponed until this work was done? Or doesn't this contest matter to you?"

"It matters," I said, placing my purse on a nearby table. I reached for the zipper. Now would be a good time to lighten the load.

Robbee waved some eucalyptus, filling the air with its medicinal odor. "You couldn't prove it by your actions. I'd like the chance to run all over Branson, too, but one of us was needed here."

"I'm here now, so stop being a grouch." Given Robbee's mood, I left my purse alone and pushed up my sweater sleeves. "What can I do to help?"

"I've processed the flowers, and I'm almost finished dividing them into groups for the contestants. If I haven't done it right, you'll have to take over."

I stared at him. Something was bugging him besides my being gone. "Spit it out, Robbee," I said. "What's really hacked you off?"

His laugh was bitter. "Being alone this morning gave me

plenty of time to think about what an ass I was not to have applied myself at the semifinals." He plopped the eucalyptus into a bucket and picked up some purple statice. "I could be in line for a trip to Hawaii, where I'd drown my problems in the tropical atmosphere."

"Why do you want to run away?"

He looked surprised. "I'm not trying to run away. I'm just tired of the same old, same old." He stuffed the statice into the container with the eucalyptus. "I want exotic. I want to see fields of flowers waiting to be cut and shipped to the States. I want to see bougainvillea growing naturally, not planted in baskets or sheltered by a greenhouse. I want to see acres and acres of tulips in Holland, and the tropical rain forests where new species of plants are being discovered and destroyed every day."

I nodded slowly. "Yeah. It would be nice to see all the things you've mentioned, but we always have to come back to our problems."

"I could travel the rest of my life and never look over my shoulder. I doubt that anyone in town would notice if my shop were closed. I say I own the business, but the bank has a larger investment. If I don't do something soon, I'll lose what little equity I have."

I'd been looking for a way to introduce Stephanie's name into a conversation. This was the opening I needed. "Is that why you were interested in Stephanie McDuffy's artwork? Did you think her pictures would bail you out of a floundering business?"

Robbee's hand hovered over a bucket of red carnations. "How do you know about Stephanie's artwork? Did she sell you pictures before she died?"

"I don't own any of her work, but I've seen it, and it's incredible. How did you meet her?"

His movements were jerky as he counted twenty-four carnations and dropped them into a bucket. "I was in the process of telling you last night when Delia cut me off. What difference does it make now?"

"No difference," I lied. "I just thought we'd visit while we finished these chores."

My answer must have sounded feasible because Robbee said, "It was in June at the Fleur-De-Lis Extravaganza. Stephanie was a . . . uh . . . rather hefty woman. She stepped on my foot while we were waiting in line to take the tour bus up to the conservatory. We started a conversation, and when she discovered I was a florist, we had plenty to talk about."

"Her parents are here in Branson." I hesitated. This was always the hard part—the leading questions, the tweaking with the truth, but I consoled myself that it was for a good cause. "I understand that you had a nice chat with them in the lobby."

"Me? I never talked to the McDuffys. I didn't even know they were here."

It had the ring of truth. "Oh, getting back to Stephanie. Besides going to the lily show, what else did she do?"

Robbee stared at me. "What's the deal, Bretta? This doesn't sound like a visit to me. It's more of an interrogation."

"I guess it is. Mr. and Mrs. McDuffy have asked me to find out what upset their daughter when she was in Branson last June. Since you'd met her, I thought you might offer up a solution or two."

"Upset? How?"

"I'm not sure. That's what I'm trying to find out."

"She didn't seem upset to me. Stephanie and I shared an interest in plants and flowers, and that's what we talked about. We spent several hours together at the conservatory, and then we had a nice supper here at the hotel. I can't imagine why her being upset almost a year ago should matter when the woman is dead. But you might ask Darren or Gellie if they know anything more."

I gasped. "Darren or Gellie?"

"Darren was the featured speaker at the conservatory. Gellie was taking the tour the same day Stephanie and I were there. She and Stephanie visited while I went to see the Fern Grotto. That's my favorite spot in the conservatory. It's peaceful with water cascading over a thirty-foot rock formation. When I stand at the base of that waterfall, I can imagine I'm on some tropical island. The air is thick with mist, and—"

"What about the rest of our group? Were any of them on this tour?"

Irked at my interruption, Robbee snapped, "I told you last night that most of us that were at the introductory dinner were also at the lily show. Miriam was there, but she was too snobbish to speak to us. Zach was strutting his stuff. Bernice was trailing Tyrone, but I didn't see Delia, Chloe, Effie, Allison, or you, for that matter."

Lavelle had said that Stephanie was "changing for a man she'd just met." I studied Robbee's handsome face. "Did you come on to Stephanie? Did you make her feel special?"

"How do I know how she felt?"

A line from Vincent's note came to mind: *She'd sit in her room, sip tea, listen to the music, and wait impatiently for the mail to arrive.* "Did you mail her presents? Send her letters? Did you kiss her?"

"Kiss her!" Robbee jerked in surprise. "Hell no. This wasn't a romance, Bretta. I was hoping to buy her artwork for my shop, not get her in the sack."

"So you didn't lead her on?"

"I shook her hand when I left." He ducked his head. "Well, I did press my lips to her wrist, but it didn't mean anything."

I couldn't hide my disgust. Robbee's flirtatious manner was as natural to him as breathing. I'm sure he was telling the truth when he said his kiss to Stephanie's wrist hadn't meant anything—to him. But to a lonely young woman, who'd probably never had the attention of a handsome man, it would have meant something special.

"Don't give me that look," said Robbee. "I didn't do anything wrong."

"Then don't sound so defensive."

"I'm out of here," he said, wiping his hands on a towel. "I've done more than my share of the work." He muttered good-bye and left.

Lavelle had said that Robbee's main interest in Stephanie had been the flower pictures. He'd confirmed that, but wouldn't a part of Stephanie hope to push his attention beyond those pictures? Listening to the same recording over and over while sipping tea, and waiting for the mail sounded like the actions of a woman in love.

Did I believe Robbee when he said he hadn't flirted with Stephanie? My mouth twisted into a sour grimace. Robbee was more than capable of snagging the heart and raising the hopes of a lonely woman like Stephanie McDuffy.

In Robbee's mind he probably hadn't treated Stephanie any differently than he treated any other woman. But could his flirtation be classed as "leading her astray"? While Robbee's type of innocent dalliance could cause pain to the person who took him seriously, it was scarcely an offense that demanded punishment. Unless there was more at stake than a woman's broken heart.

The door behind me suddenly opened, and Bailey Monroe walked into the room.

Chapter Eleven

Bailey's entrance took me by surprise. I stared at him, taking note of his physical attributes. His eyes were the color of unpolished copper. His stomach flat, his chest muscular. As he moved past me, I appraised a rear that would look fine in a pair of tight jeans.

My heart pitter-pattered at the sight of him, but I quickly diagnosed my reaction as coming from the unexpected opportunity to make a few shrewd inquiries of him in general, and his reason for going to the funeral chapel in particular.

I couldn't blurt out my questions, so I finessed my way to the subject by giving him my most winsome smile. "Hi," I said. I made a sweeping gesture to the room. "As you can see the contest flowers have arrived."

"Colorful," was his only comment.

"I'm looking forward to the conservatory tour this afternoon," I said, maneuvering my end of the conversation. "It'll be the first time I've gotten to do something fun since I came to Branson."

He didn't say anything, but poked at the contents of a box of leather leaf fern. I was ready to swing into what he'd been doing that morning. "I saw you leave the hotel and get into a truck. Did you take that drive up into the hills that you invited me to—"

Before I could finish, Bailey foiled my attempt at subtlety by interrupting, "Are these all the flowers?"

I raised my eyebrows. Most people would've been bowled over by the accumulated mass. "How many do *you* think we need?"

He shrugged and moved to the door that led into the room with the walk-in cooler. He cocked his head. "More in there?"

"Not many. We used most of them in arrangements for the conference display. These flowers are for the contest." I tried again, using another tact. "I read in the morning paper that a couple was found dead at the bottom of a ravine."

Bailey's expression didn't change.

"The information was sketchy. I wonder who they were?"

He turned on his heel and went into the other room. I followed, and knew that my control over the situation had vanished, if I'd had it in the first place, which I doubted. Bailey had come downstairs for a reason and feeding me information wasn't on his agenda.

He switched on the light and tugged open the cooler door.

"What are you looking for?" I asked. In this area I could be blunt, too.

"Honeysuckle."

"You won't find any here. I've never seen it used as a cut flower because the vase life would be too short. Why do you want honeysuckle?"

"Butterflies love it. Which of these flowers are the most fragrant? We need some to make a display upstairs."

"You're building a display now? I thought your conference started yesterday. Why didn't your committee think of flowers before they came to Branson?"

He looked over his shoulder at me. "Is everything with your conference going perfectly?"

"I live in hope," I said dryly. His lips twitched with humor, and I grinned. When he continued to stare into my eyes, I shifted my gaze. The impulses running through my body were unnerving.

I cleared my throat. "The . . . uh . . . stargazer lilies are the most fragrant, but they're also the most expensive. I can't give them away."

"Money," said Bailey softly. "It always comes back to money, doesn't it?"

This man could rile me faster than a telemarketer, but being near him made my heart thump in an abnormal fashion. "I wasn't talking about being compensated. The flowers aren't mine to give away or to sell. They were donated to the association for our contest."

Bailey pulled a fifty-dollar bill from his pocket and pressed it into my hand. "I don't know of any organization that can't use extra cash. I'd like five pink carnations, a stem of lilies, and some of that stuff over there." He pointed to the glossy foliage that had arrived from California last night. "I like the shiny leaves."

His random choices went against my creative nature. "That foliage is too heavy to use with the flowers you've chosen. How about some baby's breath, or maybe some fern to give your bouquet an airy look?"

Bailey snorted. "I'm going to stuff the flowers into a water pitcher and set it on a table with literature about attracting butterflies to gardens. Do you think anyone will care if the greens are heavy or if the bouquet is airy?"

"They should," I said as I stepped past him into the cooler. I broke off a woody stem of greenery, then came out of the cooler, shutting the door a bit harder than necessary. I chose the carnations and the lily, then looked around for something to wrap them in.

Bailey took the flowers out of my hands. "Thanks," he murmured and buried his nose in the open lily blossom. "These *are* strong smelling," he said, looking at me over the tops of the blooms.

I smothered a giggle. The rusty-brown pollen from the anther had left its imprint across the tip of his nose. I touched one of the anthers, and then showed him the dust on my finger. "You look like a brown-noser," I said softly. "A good cop would never want to be accused of that."

Bailey laid the flowers on a table. In a measured tone, he said, "I told you I was a deejay."

"That's right, you did say that. My radar must be on the fritz."

Bailey took a step closer. "You need something else to think about," he said, cupping my head in his hands. He leaned forward and rubbed his nose sensuously across mine.

Our breath mingled. Our eyes locked. Nerve endings exploded all over my body, and then his lips touched mine. His kiss was as soft and light as the brush of a rose petal. He stepped back, picked up his flowers, and walked out.

When I could breathe again, I murmured, "Oh, Carl, I'm sorry."

"Why, Babe, because you enjoyed a little kiss?"

"But I don't even know the man."

Carl's derisive laughter rang in my ears. "What's to know? Bailey Monroe intrigues you."

"More like irritates and aggravates. Effie was right. Bailey's a cop. I could kick myself for not seeing it sooner. My gosh, I lived with you for twenty-four years, I ought to be able to spot one."

Staring off into space, I mused aloud, "I wonder if anything Bailey told me is the truth. When we spoke on the elevator, he said he was an avid gardener. Wouldn't an experienced gardener know about the pollen on the lily? Wouldn't he know which flowers were the most fragrant? Why didn't he go to the roses or the carnations or the lilies without asking me?"

"He wanted honeysuckle, Babe."

I grimaced. "That's a moot point. Everyone knows honeysuckle has an aroma. When I didn't have what he wanted, wouldn't an avid gardener and a butterfly enthusiast know which flowers to pick?

"Effie told him I'd lost pounds and pounds. So why did he make that crack about fat women to me? Gellie was right to worry about packing on the pounds. My emotions are a direct line to my overeating. I think I'm strong, but, Carl, there are so many pressures.

"And speaking of pressures, what about the McDuffys? Is Robbee involved in their deaths? Did Stephanie witness something at the hybrid lily exhibition that haunted her? Lavelle said she had been filled with hopes and dreams when she came home. Was Robbee the main focus of those hopes and dreams?"

I sighed a gusty breath. "It looks like I have plenty of suspects, if I take into account that half our contestants and board of directors was at that June exhibit. Darren, Gellie, Miriam, Zach, Tyrone, and Bernice were all on that tour. How does this floral conference factor into what's going on?"

I waited expectantly for one of Carl's intelligent commentaries, but he was silent. Grumpily, I reached for the switch to the lights just as the phone rang. I picked up the receiver and said, "Basement. This is Bretta."

"I have information on the McDuffys."

The voice was raspy. I couldn't tell if it was a man or a woman. "Who is this?"

"You want what I have or not?"

"How do you know the McDuffys?"

"I'm hanging up."

"All right, all right. What kind of information do you have?"

"I'm not going into it over the phone."

"And I'm not meeting you in some dark, deserted alley. You can keep your info—"

"Just shut up and listen. I've made some notes, and I'll leave the paper in the tropical plant that's by the entrance into the souvenir shop. Better not tarry too long."

"How do you—" I stopped when I heard the click in my ear. Tarry too long? Was that a threat that the info would be taken away if I didn't get there immediately?

I switched the lights off, grabbed my purse, and headed for the stairs. Taking the steps two at a time, I arrived at the door to the lobby. As I reached for the handle, I saw something that didn't look right. I leaned closer and spied a razor blade positioned where I'd been ready to grab. What had gotten my attention was the tail end of a piece of duct tape used to fasten the blade in place. The gray of the tape was a different color than the metal gray of the handle.

I was spooked. It showed in the tiny beads of sweat that gathered on my upper lip, and the way my legs weakened to the point where I had to lean against the wall for support. Now there wasn't any doubt that I was on someone's list. The phone call had been a red herring to get me up to the lobby quickly. I had done as predicted and leaped at the chance to know more about the McDuffys.

The use of the blade was maniacal, sadistic, and downright scary. When I felt that I could trust my legs to support me, I moved back to the door and carefully peeled the tape away. I wrapped the sticky stuff around the edge of the blade before putting the wad in my purse.

I reached for the handle, then hesitated. Someone was waiting in the lobby for me to come charging through the door with blood dripping from my fingers. I could pretend the blade had done its damage, and create a scene, but I didn't see how that would make me any wiser as to the identity of the culprit. Or I could go quietly up to the next floor and check out who was in the lobby and see if anyone showed any unusual interest in the stairwell door.

I decided on the second option, though the idea of creating a foot-stomping, hell-raising ruckus was tempting. I navigated the stairs to the floor above, eyed the handle to see if it was safe to touch, and then eased the door open wide enough so I could squeeze through. Once on the balcony, I crept to the railing and peeked over the side.

People were circulating, chatting, and enjoying a good time. My gaze drifted up and down the room, looking for anyone acting suspicious. After five minutes, I decided my surveillance was a bust. I hadn't spied any furtive maneuvers.

I took the elevator down to the lobby and brazenly crossed to the six-foot, multiple-stemmed rubber tree plant that was outside the souvenir shop entrance. Pushing the heavy branches this way and that, I searched among the broad leaves for the piece of paper I was sure didn't exist.

Empty-handed, I moved on to the conference room. Just my rotten luck, Bernice was the first person I met. Her expression mirrored my own grouchy mood. To put her in better spirits, I pulled Bailey's fifty-dollar bill from my pocket and handed it to her.

"Here," I said. "I had a chance to sell a few flowers for the butterfly convention." I watched her greedily palm the money. Bailey had told the truth about one thing—it always came back to money. It made people snap up and take notice. Robbee needed it to save a failing business. Bernice used it to get on the good side of Tyrone, to make him take notice of her. And Tyrone wanted this conference to show a marked increase in the association's budget.

"—enter it under donations," she was saying. "It'll help defray the cost of that trophy. Do you have any other outstanding bills?"

Wearily, I said, "No, Bernice. That's it."

"What about the box from California? Did you find a packing slip?"

"Nope. Nothing. It's just another donation."

She nodded approvingly. "Good. Good."

Keeping my voice casual, I asked, "By the way, do you know if any of the contestants or members of the board arrived earlier than Wednesday?"

"Tyrone was here Tuesday."

"He was. I wonder why?"

"Because he's concerned that this conference has a good showing. He's done a lot of work that will never give him the recognition he deserves. I think Miriam arrived on Tuesday, too. I heard her tell Allison that she needed time to herself. A day to get into a creative mode." Bernice snorted. "More like a destructive mode, if you ask me. That woman is out to cause trouble."

"You mean with the contest?"

"That among other things."

Before I could press Bernice to be more specific, she said, "I've been thinking that we should raffle off the designs after the contest. Why let the flowers go to waste? We can deposit the proceeds in the association's account."

"Money. Money. Money," I muttered under my breath. Louder, I said, "I've already told Alvin the hotel can have the arrangements to decorate the lobby."

Bernice's face flushed with anger. "You had no right to do that, Bretta. Those flowers belong to the association, and it should profit from them, not this hotel. We've paid handsomely for the use of these conference rooms. I'm taking this up with Tyrone," she said, glancing up at his room.

I followed her gaze to the second tier of rooms where Miriam and Tyrone were having a heated discussion outside his suite. Miriam's jaws were flapping. Tyrone put a hand up to stop her verbal onslaught, and she smacked him sharply across the face.

"That was slick," I said, watching Tyrone go back into his suite and the door slam shut. "Is that the kind of trouble you were talking about?"

Bernice ignored me to paddle off like a steamboat bound for rough waters.

At my elbow, Effie said, "While we were gone this morning, dear, the contest almost went to Hades in a handbasket. Judging from that scene, I'd say it's still on a downward spiral."

I glanced at Effie, and then back to Tyrone's closed door. "You know what that was about?" Effie nodded. We watched Bernice get off the elevator and plod along the balcony to Tyrone's suite. "Stupid woman," I said, shaking my head. "She doesn't have the sense God gave a goose. In the mood Tyrone is in, he just might toss her broad butt over the railing. Let's go into the conference room. We can talk there."

I led the way into the cool, dark room. Effie found the light switch and everything sprang into focus. The sight of the funeral bier made me heartsick. "I'm going to have the casket removed, Effie," I said, making a spur-of-the-moment decision.

"Because of the McDuffys, dear?"

"Yeah. I thought it would be a bit of dark humor to have Chloe lay there, then sit up to welcome the florists. Now it's too close to reality, and too painful to look at."

"You might be right. But what will you put in its place?"

"The bouquets are pretty and original. I'll set the trophy among them and let that be it. I've hid my contest notes in the bottom of the casket. If you'll help me, I'll retrieve them, and then I'll have someone from the funeral home—"

"What is it, dear?"

"I was thinking that my odds are very good that Alvin borrowed this casket from the Eternal Rest Chapel. Perhaps I can have a chat with whoever comes to pick it up."

"When will you find the time? Don't forget the conservatory tour is in an hour. We have the Mel Tillis show tonight." Her tone held a light rebuke. "Other people are depending on you, dear. Florists have been trickling in all morning. I know the McDuffys' deaths are a personal concern, but don't slight our conference and contest."

"I'm trying, but what did you mean that the contest was going to hell in a handbasket?"

"Hades, dear. I don't use that other word. I wanted to talk about what happened at last night's dinner on our trip this morning, but you had plenty on your mind."

"What happened?"

"After you left the dining room, Miriam tried to draw Darren into a conversation about some recent flower designs he'd done for a wedding and the grand opening of a new theater here in Branson. She pressed him relentlessly about his work. Then as we were leaving the dining room, I heard her tell Tyrone that the poop was about to splatter." Color tinged Effie's cheeks. "I've cleaned that statement up, too, dear."

"I'm still not getting it, Effie. What does that have to do with the contest?"

"When we returned from our morning jaunt, I planned to rest, but I found a message on my door. Tyrone had summoned his board of directors for a meeting. Allison, Bernice, and I gathered in his room, where he announced that Delia has hurt her hand and is gone. Tyrone told us that since Miriam was so enthralled with what Darren had accomplished with his designs, then others would be, too. He's thinking of canceling the contest and having Darren put on a one-man show."

My chin came up. "He can't do that."

"I'm afraid he can, though it won't make him the most popular man in this hotel. The scene we witnessed between him and Miriam is only the beginning."

"I have half a notion to go see him myself, but nothing would be accomplished."

"There's more, dear."

My mouth dropped open. I quickly recovered and sighed. "Lay it on me. I might as well hear it all."

"Forewarned is forearmed, though in this instance, I'm not sure what you can do. It's your friend, Angelica."

"What's wrong with her?"

"Allison told me Angelica has locked herself in her room. I knew you were busy in the basement, so I tried talking to her, but she wouldn't open the door. She was sobbing so hard I could barely understand what she was saying. But it sounds as if she's fallen in love, and the man doesn't feel the same."

"Did she say that?"

"No, dear, I'm drawing conclusions. She kept muttering that 'life isn't fair' and something about 'grazing the field' and having to 'get control of my life.' " Effie clicked her tongue. "Before I left, she said 'the best place for me is home.' That's what I meant about going to Hades in a handbasket. What if Angelica drops out of the contest, too?"

Chapter Twelve

I didn't try to answer Effie's question, and as it turned out I didn't need to. In the lobby, a flood of conference attendees had arrived, but none of them was more charismatic than Gellie. Dressed in a navy-blue suit, she looked classy with a red carnation pinned to the lapel of her jacket.

I tried to gauge the expression in her eyes to see if she was putting on a front, but she appeared to be genuinely happy. Whatever had bothered her earlier had resolved itself or she'd put it behind her. She whirled and preened, showing off her new figure to a group of admirers, soaking up compliments like floral foam absorbs water.

Robbee and Chloe shared a table in the lounge. Effie had joined Bernice near the reservation desk, and both were visiting with the new arrivals. Tyrone's welcoming committee was complete when Allison joined the rest of the board. The vice president looked around the room, searching the numbers to make sure we were in attendance, as Tyrone had requested. She frowned until she spotted me. Nodding sharply, she turned to greet another newcomer.

My gaze circled the room again and would have slid on by Robbee's table, but Chloe gestured to me. I forced a polite smile to my lips and walked over. "Quite a crowd," I remarked.

"It's just fabulous," she said. "I still can't believe that I'm going to be standing before this group of florists doing original designs. I hope my brain doesn't freeze."

Being the dutiful mother figure, I said what was expected. "You'll do fine."

Chloe cast Robbee a quick glance. "Is it true that Delia has dropped out of the contest? I heard the news a few minutes ago and told Robbee. He said you hadn't mentioned it. I told him you might not know."

"I know."

Robbee swung his head up to stare at me. For a moment, his handsome features twisted into a dark scowl. That look vanished, and he flashed an irresistible smile. "If you need a replacement, I'm always available."

"We'll have to see." I moved away from their table in hopes of having a brief word with Gellie. I wanted to make sure she was all right, but I also wanted to discuss Stephanie McDuffy. I caught Gellie's eye and motioned for her to come closer. She nodded and started in my direction, but got detoured by another well-wisher. She flashed me an apologetic smile. I winked, deciding I could talk to her later.

Since I couldn't question Gellie, I settled on Darren. He was seated on a sofa, reading a magazine, ignoring the curious glances of his fellow florists. Tyrone wouldn't approve of this boorish attitude. I walked over to Darren and perched on the arm of the chair that was across from him.

"You're not mingling," I said.

Darren's expression was sullen as he looked up at me, then raised his gaze to the second level of the hotel. "He's a righteous ass."

I chuckled. "Since you've got a minute, I'd like to ask you

about a lily show you attended here at the conservatory back in June."

Darren relaxed against the sofa's overstuffed cushion. "Great show, and from what I understand, past attendance records were broken. Plus the hybrid lilies were absolutely exquisite."

"So I heard. What I'm wondering is if you remember meeting a woman by the name of Stephanie McDuffy?"

Darren rubbed his chin. "Seems familiar. What's she look like?"

"Big woman. Dark hair, sad eyes."

"Is she a florist?"

"No, but she presses flowers for pictures."

"Yeah. Yeah. I remember." He glanced across the room to Robbee. "Our token Lothario was all over her."

I leaned closer. "You mean physically?"

"No. Just charming, attentive. I wondered what the attraction was. She was pretty, if you looked directly into her face. But frankly, when a woman tops two hundred pounds, I back off." Realizing how prejudiced he sounded, and who he was speaking to—a woman who had once more than topped two hundred pounds—he dropped his gaze and muttered, "Maybe she had a glandular problem. I heard her tell Gellie that before she grazed, she'd have to think long and hard."

"Grazed?" I repeated. Before I could question Darren further, I saw Miriam get off the elevator and take a quick look around the lobby. I figured she was hunting me so she could blather about Delia leaving and about the contest categories.

I wasn't in the mood and beat a hasty retreat. I soon saw I'd made a mistake. Miriam wasn't interested in me. When she spied Darren, she smoothed her red hair and hurried to him.

She spoke, he looked up in surprise. After hesitating, he shrugged and gestured to the cushion beside him. Miriam promptly sat down, talking and waving her hands until my stomach tightened with apprehension.

The hotel's use of massive tropical plants added to the decor, and made a screened effect around the pieces of furniture. I reversed the direction I'd been traveling to the bushy schefflera plant that was directly behind the sofa occupied by Miriam and Darren. The plant would offer an excellent place to monitor what appeared to be a very animated conversation.

Before I had the chance to get into position, I met Alvin, who looked harassed. Taking pity on the poor guy, I sympathized, "Are the 'glitches' getting to you?"

"Nah, I can handle it, but you florists are a rowdy bunch." He nodded across the lobby to the Missouri Order of Butterfly Watchers' information booth. Two ladies sat behind a table, and their expressions weren't favorable as they studied the new arrivals to the hotel. "They've got their noses out of joint because your group has such a great turnout. I'm on my way to the kitchen to get them a snack. I figure a plate of brownies might sweeten up their dispositions."

"You can't feed the world," I said, but I wasn't sure if he heard. He'd moved on, disappearing into the throng. Sighing, I turned my attention back to Miriam and Darren. They appeared to be having a friendly chat. I glanced at the butterfly table.

Hmm? Butterflies and Bailey.

Where was he? Not in the lobby. I checked the balconies at each floor. No sign of him. I looked at the floral designers seated on the sofa. Miriam was up to something, but I hoped Darren could take care of himself. At the moment, Bailey was a top priority.

I sauntered over to the butterfly table, hoping for more info than when the next swallowtail swooped into Missouri. "Hi! My name's Bretta Solomon."

Both women looked up. One wore a pink-striped shirt. The other a T-shirt with a huge monarch butterfly plastered across her buxom bosom. "Are you interested in butterflies?" she asked.

"Oh, yes," I gushed with what I hoped was the right note of enthusiasm. "They're such dainty, exquisite little beauties. I have a garden back home, and I want to enhance it with plants that will attract the . . . uh . . . little . . . beauties. Bailey Monroe told me to drop by your table."

The women looked at each other. "Monroe?" asked pink-striped shirt. "Is he a new member? I don't recognize the name."

In spite of myself, I gave a glowing physical description of Bailey. When I was finished, pink-striped shirt said, "That sounds like the man who donated the flowers." She pointed to the bouquet sitting on the floor. "It was a nice idea, but too top heavy for the water pitcher. We need a vase, but no one has offered us one."

I could have taken the hint, but her tone put me off. "Bailey is so thoughtful and tenderhearted, too. He was very upset about those butterflies that were captured yesterday and subsequently died. He and the president of your organization were going to mount the bodies on a poster as a reminder to other members to be more careful." I made a show of looking around their area. "I don't see the poster. Isn't it finished?"

Ms. Butterfly Bust frowned. "I'm the president, and I don't know anything about a poster. And as to the butterflies, this is April. There aren't any butterflies here in Missouri, unless you count the ones in pupa stage, and they won't hatch until the days get warmer. Strong winds will blow different species into our state, but not until we get breezes from the south. That won't be for another four to eight weeks, if you can count on our weather, which you can't."

"I . . . uh . . . must have misunderstood. But you do know Bailey?"

"We can't know every member personally." Pink-striped shirt smiled proudly. "We're eight hundred members strong."

I persisted. "But Bailey is one of your members?"

With her butterfly jiggling, the one in the T-shirt pulled a notebook from a briefcase that was sitting on the chair behind them. She flipped the pages. "Monroe. Monroe. Here it is. Blair Monroe. No, wait. You said Bailey. Nope, don't have a Bailey Monroe listed."

Suddenly there was a loud cheer from the lobby. I looked over my shoulder. Gellie was on board a baggage cart, and a harassed porter wheeled her down a ramp. She smiled and waved like a queen, having the time of her life, while her colleagues applauded.

"From the moment that woman got off the elevator, she's been creating a ruckus," said Ms. T-shirt disapprovingly. "I hope they quiet down before evening. I need my rest."

I tried not to roll my eyes. "They're excited at seeing each other. I'd better get back to my duties. Have a good conference," I said as I walked away.

It was rewarding to know I'd been right that Bailey had lied about being a member of the Missouri Order of Butterfly Watchers. I also suspected that he wasn't telling the truth about being an avid gardener. He'd shown an interest in the flowers, wandering around the basement. I started to grin at the memory of the pollen on his nose, but stopped when that thought recalled the brush of his lips against mine.

"Don't go there," I murmured, ignoring the flip-flop of my stomach.

Doubling around another grouping of chairs, I came upon the schefflera plant. Quickly I stooped to tie my shoelace while straining my ears.

Miriam was saying, "My daughter, Teresa, can take a piece of cloth and with a few snips of her scissors and a needle and thread whip up an outfit that can take your breath away." The back of the sofa bulged, as Miriam shifted her position. "Teresa's head is full of clever ideas. So often she can't sleep at night, and has to get up and sketch the designs so she doesn't forget them."

"She shouldn't put her ideas on paper," said Darren. "I never commit anything to a physical drawing. When I need an idea, the design in my head is transferred to my hands. I'm fortunate that my fingers instinctively know what to do."

Ho hum, I thought, such titillating conversation. I was ready to move on when I heard my name. "Bretta's being obstinate about these secret contest categories, but I'm not surprised. Doesn't it bother you not knowing what to expect?"

"Of course not," denied Darren with a short laugh. "I've designed arrangements for dignitaries all over the world. I can surely please this competition. My repertoire suits any occasion."

"I wish Teresa had your confidence. She's a behind-the-scenes person."

"Confidence is the name of the game. A shy designer won't make it in this competitive world. You have to flaunt your work with an aggressive attitude if you're going to be noticed."

"How fortunate that you were blessed with both an outgoing personality and creative talent. My daughter lacks the confidence to present her ideas to the right people. You wouldn't be shy at offering your ideas for, say, a complete renovation of this lobby. What if your customer wanted art nouveau? What would you do?"

"Do?" repeated Darren sharply.

"I'm curious how your creative mind works. Take that corner for instance. If you could redesign that atrocious silk arrangement, what would you change?"

A pair of shiny penny loafers appeared beside me. I knew those shoes, and wondered again why dimes were in the slots? Reluctantly, I lifted my gaze to a well-creased trouser leg, followed by a crisp-white shirt and neatly knotted tie. Finally, I settled on a countenance that made my heart hammer.

Bailey jerked his head, indicating that I was to follow him. Sighing softly, I crept from behind my screen of foliage to the alcove where he waited.

"That must've been one helluva knot in your shoelace," he said dryly. "You were hunkered behind that plant for a good five minutes."

Why was Bailey watching me? And where had he been? I'd searched the lobby and the balconies before I'd gone to the butterfly information tables. Had he seen me talking to those ladies? Did he know I'd been checking up on him?

My cheeks felt hot. In an attempt to hide my embarrassment, my tone was waspish. "Don't you have butterflies to catch or mount or whatever it is you enthusiasts do?" He drilled me with a hard stare, but I continued undaunted. "Or as an *avid gardener*, maybe you're hanging around for the conservatory tour?"

"Is that what *you're* doing?"

Before I could answer, Darren jumped up from the sofa and raced for the elevator. When he saw the long lines, he detoured to the stairs. I looked back at Miriam. She gazed up at Tyrone, who was at the second-floor railing. Her satisfied smile made me quake and made him disappear into his suite.

The way I saw it, I had three choices. I could go to Miriam and ask for an explanation. I could talk to Tyrone, or I could try to calm Darren. I settled on the latter.

"Gotta go," I said to Bailey, and started away.

"That conservatory tour sounds like a good idea. I think I'll accompany you, and we'll call it our first date."

First date? That put the brakes on. I glanced around with a frown. Bailey's lips curved into a grin that didn't quite reach his eyes. They remained cool and steady on me.

"Eavesdropping can get you into serious trouble," he said, clasping my hand and tucking it firmly into the crook of his arm. "You need someone to keep you out of trouble."

When I opened my mouth to protest, he calmly patted my wrist. "No need to thank me. I'll be at *your* side when we get on that bus."

For some reason his last remark struck me as a warning. Add to that his unrelenting grip on my hand, and the fact that he'd been watching me before he'd drawn my attention away from Darren and Miriam, and I got the distinct impression that I was being herded into a corner.

I glanced around the crowded lobby, wondering how many witnesses there would be if I made a scene. Effie, Allison, and Bernice were headed toward the café but had craned their necks to gawk in our direction. Chloe and Robbee were studiously appraising Bailey and me. When Robbee caught my eye, he winked slowly. I pursed my lips. I'm sure it would ease his conscience if he thought I was having a steamy affair with Bailey. I could hardly point a finger at his dallying if I was partaking of a bit of my own.

I looked up at Bailey and found his gaze on me. "What are you staring at?" I asked, feeling the heat rise in my cheeks again. Only this time embarrassment wasn't the stimulus.

"I'm just trying to figure you out."

"Are you sure you have the time, what with your extracurricular activities?"

Bailey's eyes crinkled at the corners. "Time is all I've got, Bretta."

I gulped but managed to say, "I need a drink." Since he still had a grip on my hand, I towed him toward the terrace lounge, choosing a table well away from Robbee.

As I sat down, I asked, "I assume you're buying?" When Bailey nodded, I said, "In that case, I'll have diet Coke, a Reuben sandwich, and a slice of coconut cream pie."

Bailey's eyebrows rose almost to his hairline. I smiled sweetly. "I always eat when I'm happy, worried, or upset."

"And which are you?" he asked, stroking my fingers.

"None of the above. Just hungry." I pulled my hand away. "It's been a busy morning."

Bailey accepted my answer with a grin and gave the order to the waiter.

I tried to settle back in my chair. I didn't expect Bailey to admit that he was a cop, especially if he was on assignment. But I was interested in Bailey as a man. Was he a gardener? Did we have that much in common?

I'm not into memorizing the botanical names of plants, but

I knew a couple from having done some research regarding my garden back home. Once the waiter had left, I said, "This might prove to be an instructive afternoon. As an avid gardener, you can point out some of the more interesting species of plants. On the ride up to the conservatory, I'm hoping to see some *Cercis canadensis*."

Casually, I propped my elbow on the table. "Don't you just love their blossoms? But nothing can compare to the *Cornus florida*. Which is your favorite?"

Without missing a beat, Bailey answered, "The *Cornus florida*. I used to live in Tallahassee, so I have a good association with that species of plant."

I felt a stab of disappointment. The *Cercis canadensis* is the common redbud tree. The *Cornus florida* is Missouri's state tree, the flowering dogwood. Bailey didn't have to know these names to be a gardener, but why did he feel the need to bluff an answer? I could have called him on his mistake, but what the hell? I had the rest of the afternoon to figure this man out.

Chapter Thirteen

"Haversham Hall is the pride and product of coal baron Samuel F. Haversham," said the tour guide, standing on the front steps of the estate. "A meager upbringing left its mark on Samuel, and once his fortune was made, he left Virginia to settle here in the Ozarks. Having spent his younger days in mine shafts, he opted to live his remaining years high on this hillside, surrounded by nature's rare beauty."

"That accounts for all the glass used in this conglomerate," remarked Bailey in my ear. "I'd want plenty of sunlight, too, if I'd spent time underground."

His warm breath sent a shiver down my spine. I forced my attention to the tour guide. The young woman, who'd introduced herself as Joan, surveyed her audience.

"You'll have to excuse me," she said in a choked tone, "but this part of the tour always brings a lump to my throat."

Behind me, Bailey pressed closer and put a hand on my arm. I glanced up at his profile, but his eyes were on the tour guide, absorbing every word.

"I'm sure all of you can imagine Samuel's joy at owning such splendor, and his pleasure at feasting his eyes on this wondrous view." Joan smiled tearfully at our group. "And now you have that same opportunity."

"For a damned stiff price," grumbled Bernice. "You'd think we could've gotten a better deal since we're staying at the hotel."

Our tour group was fifty-five strong, and I stood within arm's reach of Bernice. When heads turned in our direction, I wanted to punch her. I would've settled for distancing myself, except Bailey had penned me in. He was at my elbow, blocking my migration to a more desirable location.

I pulled myself away from any physical contact. I tried to remain neutral, but it was difficult to ignore the attraction I felt toward him. As the tour guide droned on, I ridiculed myself for being sucked in by Bailey's physical allure. A compliment or two, a light stroke of his fingers, and I was fascinated.

I pulled in a breath of air and got a snootful of Old Spice cologne. The aroma was reminiscent of the romance that was gone from my life but not forgotten. A powerful wave of longing lapped at my senses. I missed the lingering kisses, the cuddling on the couch, and the giggling in the dark when that strategic spot behind my knee is caressed.

I had misgivings—even suspicions—about this man, and yet I had flights of fancy whenever he touched me. Even now, I dropped my gaze and studied his fingers—long and slender, the nails blunt cut. I turned my head away. Instead of letting him beguile me, I should be asking him questions, stimulating him with *my* charms, if I still had any and could remember how to use them.

Since we'd left the hotel, he'd acted the infatuated suitor—holding doors, smiling when our eyes met, touching my arm briefly to point out a particular vista. As I entered the house with Bailey on my heels, I identified with Samuel Haversham's need for space. I made as if to reach into my pocket and dug my elbow into Bailey's ribs. His grunt caused my lips to twitch, but my expression was virtuous when I murmured, "Sorry." He nodded but took a step back.

Joan droned on about the forty-eight windows, which afforded a panoramic view. Ordinarily I'd have been taking mental notes of my surroundings. I'd have noticed the furnishings and accessories in each room. Seen how the draperies, upholstered furniture, and pieces of art accentuated the colors of the walls. My mind was otherwise occupied.

Bailey's comment about fat women still bothered me. Statistics show anyone who loses weight stands a good chance of gaining it back. I pictured all those shrunken little fat cells waiting under my skin for a spree of overeating so they could puff up again. Bailey had admitted, "Fat women annoy the hell out of me." So why was he being so damned attentive to a potential fat woman?

I glanced at him, and he flashed me a smile. My lips tipped up weakly. He was handsome and interesting in a mystifying way. He represented the unknown, which to my inquisitive nature was the equivalent of an unexpected gift. I was distracted from the tour, but attracted to finding out more about Bailey.

I hung back from the group, pretending a curiosity for an odd piece of statuary. "This is different," I said, pointing to the atrocity. The hunk of stone had been chipped and hollowed into a contortion of geometric shapes. "I wonder what it means?"

"Our guide said it was done by a local artist. We could look him up and ask."

"That's not necessary," I said, though the idea of spending time driving around with Bailey was tempting. "But the sculpture is strange, and makes me wonder what the artist was trying to say. Life has enough oddities. Take for instance the way we met." I turned a dazzling smile on Bailey, but he didn't see it. He was gazing up at the intricate plaster cornices and elaborate carved wood moldings. I persevered. "We met in an elevator. Some people might see that as an indication of how our friendship might progress—highs, lows, ups, and downs."

"These old houses fascinate me," said Bailey. "I'd love to own one and renovate it, but I don't think I'd have the nerve to open it to the public."

I wanted to get a personal conversation going. I tried again, pausing at a window. "Last fall I became the proud owner of an eighteen-room mansion. Do you live in an apartment or a house?"

"The tour is going upstairs. Shouldn't we catch up with them?"

I dug in my heels. I wanted just one straight answer. "Well? Do you live in an apartment or a house?"

Bailey shrugged. "I keep a roof over my head. Are we taking the rest of the tour or not?"

"What do *you* want to do?"

"I'm with you."

"Don't you have a preference?"

"Not really."

"Why did you come?"

"Why not?"

I wanted to pull my hair out by the roots. To calm myself, I took a couple of breaths. "Why don't you take the tour, and I'll just hang around down here by the conservatory?"

"I'll hang, too."

How could one man be so totally annoying? "You stay. I'm leaving." I walked off grumbling.

"You'll have to speak up if I'm going to answer," said Bailey, keeping pace at my side.

"Answer? That's a novel idea."

As we approached a public rest room, the door opened and Gellie walked out. Her jaws were grinding away on something until she caught sight of us but mainly me. She wouldn't meet my gaze and quickly swallowed whatever was in her mouth.

I recognized the look of guilt on her face. That expression coupled with her jaw activity told me she'd sneaked a forbidden treat. "Are you okay?" I asked.

Gellie turned her head away. "Potty break," she mumbled.

Conscious of Bailey at my back, I said quietly, "Effie says you were upset earlier." I smiled sympathetically and leaned closer. "If you're tempted to overeat, just give me a call, and I'll talk you out of it. That's what friends are for."

She gave me a horrified look and practically ran down the hall. I watched as she maneuvered herself to the front of the tour, where she was well away from me.

Without a word to Bailey, I went into the rest room. There were three stalls, all unoccupied. I glanced in each doorway, then went to the wastebasket that was sitting by the sink. On top of the trash were two Butterfinger candy bars—unopened.

What had Gellie been eating? I reached under the bars and saw an empty plastic bag. I pulled it out, and down in a corner saw a speck of green that was half the size of a dime. I worked the particle out of the bag and into the palm of my hand, where I pressed it with a fingernail.

Good for Gellie. She'd tossed the candy away and had eaten something healthful. I frowned. Then why had she acted flustered at being caught?

I put the bit of vegetation back in the bag and tucked it in my purse. After washing my hands, I came out of the rest room to find Bailey waiting for me. The tour group had disappeared. "You should have gone on," I said.

"Who was that woman?" asked Bailey. "She was creating quite an uproar in the hotel lobby. From what I gathered she's lost a bunch of weight. How'd *she* do it?"

"I guess she closed her mouth and got up off her wide behind." I waited for his reaction at my use of his insensitive comment, but he only stared at me in stony silence. "I'm going to pass on the rest of the house tour," I said, walking off.

I took the necessary twists and turns through the maze of hallways until I was at the back of the house. Glancing over my shoulder, I saw I'd lost Bailey. I stepped through the door marked EMPLOYEES' LOUNGE and surprised a man and a woman in a hot clinch. A little hanky-panky on the job, if I gauged their embarrassment correctly. I acted as if I hadn't noticed anything amiss and swung into what I wanted.

"I'm looking for some information about a couple I know. I understand that in the last four days Mr. and Mrs. McDuffy have taken this tour several times. Vincent is very much overweight. His wife is extremely thin. Do either of you remember them?"

The man shrugged and walked out. The woman leaned lazily against the table. She had big hair and a small body. Her skin had that bottled-bronzed look with the yellow undertones. She must have slathered the sunless suntan lotion on by the bucketful to achieve such a jaundice glow.

"I know who you mean," she said in answer to my question. "But I didn't know their name. They seemed kind of lonely and sad, and weren't interested in visiting with anyone. They never took the house tour, but sat in the conservatory and stared at the flowers, talking to each other. I bought them a couple of Cokes, and we chatted."

"Any particular subject?"

She lifted a slender shoulder. "Mostly about the plants, the flowers, and the crowds."

"And you say they didn't talk to anyone? They weren't meeting someone?"

"Not that I saw, though I think they were on the lookout."

"For anyone in particular?"

"The man asked if I knew anyone that went by the nickname of 'Friend.' I don't, but I told them that was a nicer handle than mine." She looked around, then lowered her voice. "My family calls me Saffron." She stroked her dark hair. "Isn't that ridiculous? I can't for the life of me understand where they came up with that."

I eyed her tinted skin and murmured, "Go figure." I thanked her, then headed out the door and down the hall toward the conservatory. So Mabel and Vincent were looking for someone nicknamed "Friend."

At the final stretch to the conservatory, I saw Bailey leaning against a wall, a perturbed look on his face. "Where've you been?" he asked when I was within earshot.

"Here and there," I said, sauntering past him.

Three strides and he was at my elbow. "Doing what?" he demanded.

"This and that." I sped up, then wished I hadn't. Robbee and Chloe were seated on one of the benches that flanked the entry into the conservatory. Chloe beckoned me.

When I got closer, she whispered, "Bretta, who is that fantastic man you're with? He's so distinguished. Makes me think of a congressman."

Wasn't that the truth? Pushy, snoopy, and full of hot air described Bailey to perfection.

"He looks irritated," said Robbee, staring behind me. "Did the two of you have words?"

I didn't bother turning around. "Very, very few."

The aroma of Old Spice cologne told me Bailey was nearby. I didn't know how close until he spoke in my ear. "Here comes the tour."

I jumped in surprise.

"Why so edgy?" he asked. "I've heard that comes from a guilty conscience. Been doing something you shouldn't?"

"Shh. I'm listening to the guide." He didn't dispute me, but his frown let me know he wasn't buying my sudden interest in Joan's commentary. Just to prove him wrong, I tuned in to what she was saying.

"—winter weather makes most of us burrow under a blanket in front of a fire," said Joan, leading the group toward us. "Samuel Haversham wanted to enjoy each season to its fullest. The main conservatory was built in 1922. Eight additional wings were constructed as interest in the collected plants blossomed."

Several people tittered politely at Joan's play on words. Bernice snorted. "More like an excuse for hiking the price of admission."

The snide remark flustered the young tour guide. Joan stammered, "We...uh...here at Haversham Hall take pride in our work and our jobs." She tried to smile, but the corners of her mouth wavered. "As I was saying, the...uh...eight additional wings have provided our staff with more landscaping space. The Desert Den contains cacti that are over one hundred years old. We've used sand and rock outcroppings taken directly from the Mojave to give our display authenticity. Our Fern Grotto has a collection of plants that came from the darkest jungles in Africa. I'm sorry that this exhibit is closed at the present, but you're welcome to sneak a peek across the barrier. We're revamping the thirty-foot waterfall, so I'll ask that none of you go beyond the designated area.

"My favorite spot to relax is the Orangery. The first known greenhouses were constructed by northern Europeans to grow oranges, a fruit exotic to their region. Even George Washington had a greenhouse at Mount Vernon. It was called a 'piney' since it was built to grow pineapples, his favorite fruit.

"At this point of the tour, you can wander on your own. You are free to go through all of the conservatories except the Fern Grotto. I . . . uh . . . want to thank you for being such a . . . uh . . . large group. Enjoy the rest of the tour." She quickly departed.

Robbee snickered. "We sure made an impression on her. Tyrone warned us to be on our best behavior. When he hears about this, he'll have Bernice so rattled she won't know her 'assets' from a hole in the ground. I wonder why she acted like a jerk?"

Chloe flicked her fingers down Robbee's shirt. "You men are such ninnies. Bernice is crazy about Tyrone. It won't matter to her if he rakes her over the coals, just so he focuses on her, even if it's only for a few minutes."

"Seems damned stupid to me," said Robbee. "Women play the most devious games."

I glared at him. He met my gaze calmly and asked, "What was Miriam talking to Darren about? At first I thought they were getting along fine, then he turned red and stomped off."

I didn't want to let his remark slide about devious women, especially when he was such a pro, but I squelched my rebuttal. "I hope Darren is still at the hotel when we get back. He may have packed his bags and left."

"Two designers out of the contest," said Robbee, rubbing his hands together. "I may get a shot at those beaches yet."

"If Darren leaves, too, there won't be a contest."

"How can you say that?" asked Chloe. "All the florists are here and there's more coming. Even if Darren does leave the contest, we'll have to go ahead. You'll see," she said, "everything will be just fine."

Yeah. Yeah. Who wants to see fine, when they had the chance to view a genius at work? What had Darren said to Miriam? "My repertoire suits any occasion." Why did that phrase haunt me? It sounded as if—

"Are you going to stand there the rest of the afternoon or are you coming with me to see the conservatory?" asked Bailey.

I waved my hand at Robbee and Chloe to lead the way. Bailey leaned close. "Florists are a strange bunch. I thought the butterfly watchers were a flighty group, but, babe, yours has them beat."

Air swooshed out of my lungs. It was as if Bailey had punched me in the gut. I struggled for a breath. "Don't . . . ever . . . call . . . me that." I saw astonishment register on Bailey's face, but I couldn't explain.

I hurried away, blinking back tears. Of all the names Bailey could have called me, why had he hit upon "babe"? Just the sound of the word coming from another man's lips made my skin pucker with goose bumps. No one in my life had ever called me babe except Carl. We'd only been married a short time when he'd christened me with the endearment, saying I wasn't a sugar or a honey, but a babe . . . his Babe.

I wandered aimlessly, wondering which way to go to find the rest of the group. An aerial view would have shown the conservatory resembled a giant daisy, with the domed roof as the center of the flower and each of the eight greenhouses veering off like petals.

I heard laughter and headed to my right, following the sound to the Topiary Cotillion room. I had to pass the Fern Grotto, and paused at the barrier, which was only a couple of sawhorses.

The water for the falls had been turned off, leaving the moss-stained rocks exposed. Judging the size of the holes left in the soil, massive plants had been removed from the display. The roof was covered with heavy netting that shut out the sun and made the air dank and stagnated. When in operation, it would be a refreshing place to visit, with the water pouring over the rocks, splashing into the pool. But at the moment, it looked like I felt—forlorn.

Carl's nickname for me had made me feel special, made me feel loved, but more importantly, it had made me feel connected to him. I could be at my wit's end at work, the phone would ring and it would be him. Just hearing him call me "Babe," my topsy-turvy world would right itself, and I could carry on. Had that been how Stephanie had felt about Friend?

I turned my back on the ravaged Fern Grotto and stepped through the Topiary Cotillion doorway. Everyone was having a good time. Suddenly I wanted to be part of their fun. I wanted to laugh and joke and forget all the sad memories of my past, and every frustrating detail that had to do with this weekend. Here was the place to do it.

Imagery and imagination had cast this glass-enclosed chamber into a ballroom. Wire frames had been sculpted into the shapes of five couples, who were postured in humorous positions. Thriving plants—creeping fig, wandering Jew, and English ivy—grew over the frames creating flowing gowns or tailored trousers. The topiary "dancers" were so lifelike that I expected them to yank up their roots and whirl around the floor.

It takes patience and talent to trim and train the vines to follow the designated curves. But once that feat is accomplished the results are impressive, but maintenance is a never-ending job. Haversham Conservatory has a reputation for having ten of the most elaborate topiaries in the United States. But it wasn't merely the topiaries that were imposing. It was the atmosphere in which they were presented.

Topiary Cotillion was a theatrical masterpiece. I'd read in the hotel's brochure that a computer controls the light, the sound—a waltz was playing in the background—the water for the plants, and the ventilation. While the air in the Fern Grotto had been stuffy and dead, in the Topiary Cotillion it smelled of healthy plants and moist, fertile soil.

There was a particularly loud burst of applause, and I moved until I could see what was happening. Thinking it might be a show staged for our tour, I was shocked to see Gellie as the main attraction. She'd removed the red carnation from her jacket and had stuck the flower behind her ear. Bouncing from one male topiary to another, she was making a fool of herself, asking the statue to dance while sweeping her skirt in an embellished curtsy.

I got the impression that she'd been holding court for quite a while. Several people were laughing, while others, beginning to be embarrassed by her display, were slipping quietly out of the room. Walking among the topiaries was forbidden. Signs were posted everywhere. But apparently she'd slipped under the rope and was heedlessly crushing the plants that formed the dance floor.

I called to her. "Gellie, what are you doing?"

She looked around, and her face lit up. "Bretta, honey, I'm free. My life has been anchored to the ground, but now I can glide like an eagle." She skipped up to me and peered into my face. "You of all people must understand how I feel. Our extra pounds tethered us to this earth."

She would have danced away, but I grabbed her arm. "Gellie, what's wrong? You're acting strange. Come out of there before you get into trouble."

"No. You come with me, Bretta. Let's show this group how we can fly. Spread your wings, Bretta," she cried, breaking away from my grasp. "Spread your wings, and let's soar like the angels."

"Gellie, stop talking and listen to me. What's wrong? Why are you acting—"

"Acting? I'm not acting, my fine feathered friend." She roared with inane laughter. "Feathered friend? Isn't that wonderful? I have these images in my brain, Bretta, and I have to try them."

Dodging topiaries, Gellie stepped over the rope and snatched a gauzy shawl from a woman who was with our tour group. "May I borrow this?" Gellie asked. But she didn't wait for the woman's reply. After draping the cloth over her bony frame, Gellie ran from the room, jostling anyone who got in her path.

I didn't know what to do, or what Gellie might do. She was in a terrible state, and I couldn't let her go off by herself. Others must have felt the same. There was a surge for the door, and I got caught in the shuffle.

"Let me through," I pleaded. "I have to get to Gellie."

Slowly, I broke my way through the throng and into the hall. I didn't have to ask which way she'd gone. The red carnation lay crushed on the floor. Gellie's boisterous singing guided me to the doorway of the Fern Grotto, where the barrier had been pushed aside.

Bailey had caught up to me. He took my elbow and led the way through the silent tour group. Heads were tilted back, eyes were directed to the utmost rock, thirty feet above us. Gellie had taken off her shoes, climbed the structure, and was posed with her arms outspread. Off key and using only part of the words, she was singing.

"Do something, Bailey," I said. "We have to get her down before she falls."

"You stay here and try to keep her attention. I'll move around behind her."

"Gellie," I called up to her, "I didn't know you could sing." My voice creaked with strain. "What's the name of that song? It sounds familiar."

She looked down at me. "I should have learned more of the words. Friend told me it would keep my mind on track."

"Friend? Which one, Gellie? You have so many. Come down, so we can go back to the hotel."

Bailey was nearly at the top. Just a few more feet and he could grab her. Gellie shifted her position and almost fell. There were gasps of horror.

"Gellie," I screamed. "Sit down."

She rose on her toes. "My name is Angelica, Bretta. I will fly." She flapped her arms, making the shawl flutter like gossamer wings, then she leaped from the top of the water-fall.

If she made a sound as she fell, I didn't hear it. The only noise in my ears was my own high-pitched screech.

Chapter Fourteen

🌿 "Had your friend had a fight with her husband or boyfriend?" asked the officer.

I answered his question in a spiritless monotone. "Gellie didn't have a husband." Remembering Effie's comment that she thought Gellie had fallen in love, I added, "And as far as I know, there wasn't a boyfriend."

But there was someone nicknamed "Friend" lurking around. I wanted to pursue this line of thought, but my muddled brain refused to cooperate.

It helped that the officer and I were in my room at the hotel and away from the conservatory where Gellie had died. But no change of scenery could shake the image of her balanced on that rock, her arms outstretched before she plunged to her death.

When she hit the stone pool, none of us had moved. It was Bailey who'd scrambled down from the top of the waterfall and checked for a pulse. Finding none, he'd immediately urged everyone out of the Fern Grotto, myself included. He had alerted the Branson authorities from his cell phone, and hardly before the tragedy had sunk in, our group was back aboard the bus and headed for the hotel.

"Gellie?" the officer repeated, consulting his notebook. "Angelica Weston. Gellie was a nickname?"

"There's a lot of that going around," I said, then shuddered. Gellie's last words had been an admonishment to me that her name was Angelica, but in my mind she'd always be Gellie.

"Had Ms. Weston been depressed?"

"Some. She'd lost weight, but was putting a few pounds back on."

"Do you think that's why she jumped?"

"I don't know." I mopped the tears from my cheeks. "She was trying to curb her appetite. She'd come on the tour prepared with a healthy snack."

I opened my purse and saw the empty razor-blade cartridge. I hesitated for a split second. Telling this officer about the blades taped to the door handles would complicate everything. So I simply handed him the plastic bag with the sliver of green and briefly told him how I'd come by it, and how Gellie had tossed the unopened candy bars in the trash.

The look he shot me was skeptical. "Let me get this straight. You think your friend was in control because she'd fought off eating the candy bars by substituting a bunch of green stuff?" He shrugged. "In light of the fact that she jumped, I'd say it didn't work worth a damn."

He slapped his notebook shut and tucked it into his pocket. Gingerly, he picked up the plastic bag. "I'll keep this. I may have more questions, so don't leave the hotel without letting the front desk know your whereabouts." He walked out of my room shaking his head.

I was staring at the closed door when the phone rang. I didn't want to talk to anyone, but when it continued to ring, I finally picked up the receiver. "What is it?"

"Bretta?" asked Lois.

"Oh, Lois," I said, sinking onto the bed. "Something awful

has happened." The floodgates opened, and I sobbed. "Gellie's dead. She thought she could fly and jumped off a waterfall."

"Fly? Why would a woman her size think she could get off the ground?"

"She had her stomach stapled and had lost one hundred and sixty pounds, but she was gaining again. I should have taken her worries more seriously. I should have done something to help her. I was there. I saw her—fall. It was horrible, and it happened so fast. I was helpless to do anything."

"Gosh, Bretta, I don't know what to say. We are talking about the same Gellie? The one we've known for years? I can't picture a slim and trim Gellie, let alone fathom her leaping to her death."

I used the tail of my sweater to wipe away my tears. "I don't know what's going to happen. I can't imagine us going on with the conference."

"Really? But think of all the florists who will be arriving. I've talked to several today, and they're leaving for Branson as soon as they close their shops. Too late to stop them from making the trip."

We were silent, thinking our own thoughts. I finally roused myself to ask, "So what did you need? Why'd you call?"

"I received an unexpected visitor this afternoon at the flower shop." Lois paused for dramatic effect. "Our esteemed sheriff."

My shoulders slumped even lower. "That's just great. What did Sid want?"

"For starters, he says you've been back to Spencer County today. I told him I hadn't heard from you. Is he right? Have you been back?"

"Yeah, but just to the edge of the county."

"Bretta, Sid is ticked off, but not in his usual way. He seemed genuinely worried about you. What are you doing? What have you gotten mixed up in?"

"The McDuffys have been murdered, but it's too complicated to get into now. What else did Sid say?"

"This is the frightening part. He said you're very smart, and you've done some fine work in the past, but you're out of your element and out of his jurisdiction. He won't be able to help you this time." Lois's tone grew earnest. "Sid doesn't hand out compliments, and especially not where you're concerned. Whatever you're doing, please stop."

"But I'm not doing anything."

"Yes you are. You're asking questions, chatting it up with people who could be dangerous."

I shivered at the intensity in her voice. How would she react if I told her about the razor blades? "Don't talk for a minute. I need to think."

"It's your dime. I'm at the flower shop."

Carl had taught me that with detective work you grab one primary fact and run with it, even if it doesn't seem to have a connection. It was difficult centralizing my thoughts on the McDuffys and Stephanie, when my mind wanted to hopscotch back to Gellie.

I stopped chewing on my lip. But wasn't that what this was about—a connection between the McDuffys, or at least Stephanie and Gellie? There were lots of loose ends, but the one fact that leaped—I shivered—out at me was that both women had been grossly overweight.

Gellie had taken the drastic action of having her stomach stapled to reduce her intake of food, but she'd learned that she could still eat the snacks she craved, only in small amounts. Since her choices were high in calories, she'd put on a few pounds and was horrified that she might regain the lost weight.

In the café, she'd told me that she still had "the mind of a fat woman." Most people wouldn't understand how an obese person thinks. I had an advantage. While I'd never felt frantic, there had been times when I'd cried about my weight.

As a "fat woman" Gellie had been desperate to lose her extra poundage and had resorted to surgery. In the picture of Stephanie, I'd seen that same desperation to make a change.

Change?

Had Stephanie lost weight, too? If so, how had she done it?

"Are you there?" whispered Lois in my ear. "I've got something else for you."

"Mmm? What's that?"

"Something has been bothering me. You said the McDuffys had eavesdropped on your phone conversation, while I was helping them plan the flowers for their daughter's funeral. That made me think about how small the service was. That made me think about the people who did send flowers. So, while I'm not encouraging you, I do have a scrap of information. I looked up the flower orders that we did for Stephanie's service."

"Really? That was ingenious. I'll make an official sidekick out of you yet."

Lois's tone was dry. "I don't want an ounce of credit if you get into serious trouble, but here's what I found. We sent the spray of flowers for the casket, of course, but we also sent two potted plants and one cut flower bouquet. The plants were from a Baptist church and Kidwell's Greenhouse."

"So Stephanie attended church, and bought plants at her local greenhouse. Nothing helpful there. What about the cut flower bouquet? Who was it from?"

"We received the order from a shop right there in Branson. Tessa's Flowers requested a fifty-dollar arrangement of pastel colors, but no name on the card. I've been around you long enough to know the next step. Since I had the number in front of me, I called Tessa and asked who placed the order. Sorry, but it was a cash sale."

"Damn!"

"Originally, I took the order and after studying it, I recalled thinking at the time that we sure get odd messages for sympathy cards. When Mr. Chappen died I had to write, 'Wait for me at the Pearly Gates.' However, the card we put on a sympathy bouquet for Lucille Peters's service was the best. 'Ain't misbehavin' without you,' signed 'Snookie.' I understand her husband is still looking for Snookie, whoever he or she might be. But it was another cash order, so I wasn't lying when I told him I didn't know who the sender might be."

I drummed my fingers impatiently on the nightstand. "Is this going somewhere?"

"Just thought you might like to know how this card was signed."

"I thought you said there wasn't a name."

"No name, but a neat message. I think it's the title of a song. 'Whenever I Call You "Friend." ' That's kind of nice, isn't it?"

After I'd told the woman at the front desk that I was going for a drive and would be back in an hour, I went out to my car. Just before I climbed behind the wheel I saw something on the hood. The muscles in my throat tightened. This time I used a tissue to pick up the empty Schick razor-blade container.

I looked around. A few people were in the parking lot, but no one seemed particularly interested in me. My skin was cold and clammy. My knees felt hinged on both sides. I flopped into the car unable to stand a moment longer.

Once the doors were locked, I asked myself who was stalking me? Where were all those blades that were missing from the two containers I'd found? Would they turn up when I least expected them? What if someone was seriously injured when I was the intended victim? What was I to do? Who should I talk to? I felt vulnerable sitting alone in the parking lot. I started the car and pulled out on the highway.

The fresh air felt good on my face. I lowered my car window a few more inches and pressed on the accelerator. On the seat next to me was the Kenny Loggins cassette. That was my reason for getting away from the hotel, but I couldn't concentrate on the music when I was agitated over the empty razorblade box.

Carl's voice in my ear tried to soothe me. "Settle down, Bretta. Keep your cool. Someone is playing mind games."

"What am I going to do?"

"Listen to the cassette, Babe."

I nodded, but I put off slipping it in the tape deck. I wanted the volume turned up, and I also wanted out of heavy traffic so I could focus on the lyrics.

Once I'd left Branson behind, I looked for a quiet place to pull over. Several miles outside of town I happened upon a tourist rest stop with a view of Table Rock Lake. The lot was empty, which suited my purpose. I parked my car and stared at the water that was as placid as a pool of gray paint. The edges blended and bled onto the land that was slowly being shadowed by nightfall.

I put the cassette in the tape deck but didn't push the PLAY button. I leaned against the headrest and closed my eyes. My original plan was to think about Stephanie and listen to the song that according to her parents she'd played over and over. But I was so tired. My emotional day had taken a toll on my body. I was running on empty, and yet I couldn't erase the melee of images that persisted in my mind.

"Help me, Carl," I said aloud.

But it was Bailey's voice that answered, "You need something else to think about." I visualized his face, his coppery eyes, and his warm smile. I felt his lips brush mine in a tender kiss.

"No!" I shouted, then looked around to see if someone had driven up while I'd been lost in thought. I was alone.

Frustrated, I jerked upright and punched the PLAY button. I turned the volume up and Kenny Loggins's voice, accompanied by Stevie Nicks, filled the car. Straining to catch the lyrics, I mouthed the words.

I played the song to the end, then hit the REWIND button and turned the volume a notch higher. Leaning forward, I listened carefully. A third time, I poked the button to rewind the tape, and then played it again.

When the song came to its conclusion, I snapped off the player. Gellie had sung a portion of this song before she jumped to her death. The same song Stephanie McDuffy had played, while she sipped tea and waited for the mail.

Chapter Fifteen

I glanced at the clock on the dashboard. My allotted hour away from the hotel was almost gone. I started my car and pulled out on the blacktop, traveling the dark and winding road back into Branson.

What did the Kenny Loggins song represent? I'd listened to the lyrics, but they hadn't carried any particular message. Other than the word "Friend" in the title, I couldn't see how the music was important except that it was another bond between Gellie and Stephanie. But wasn't it trivial? Kind of like a weed in a flowerbed. If I yanked it out, what difference would it make to the overall picture?

I smiled. Maybe that's what I should do to this entire investigation. Yank out the nonessential and concentrate on the basic design of my garden. I'd told Effie that I needed to discover "why" the McDuffys had been murdered. If I could do that, the guilty party would slither out of hiding.

The "why" was in my peripheral vision, but it was obscured by too many irrelevant details. I needed to pull a few more "weeds." I thought a moment. Or maybe, I needed to attack the situation from another angle. Forget the "why" and think of the "who."

Who among the suspects would call himself "Friend"?

Robbee topped the list, but I came up with more reasons for

him *not* being the suspect than I did for him. While Robbee might act like a friend, his charm was blatant and superficial. Gellie would've seen through his shallow demeanor, even if Stephanie hadn't. Robbee had answered my questions about Stephanie readily enough. He'd even offered up Gellie's name when I'd persisted in wanting to know more.

No, I was looking for someone craftier than Robbee, someone subtler, with a motive other than getting hold of Stephanie's artwork. However, before I plucked Robbee from my garden, I wanted to talk with him again.

When I entered the city limits cars were bumper to bumper, waiting to turn into the different country music theaters. Fidgeting with my rearview mirror, I watched a couple of patrol officers trying to ease the snarl of traffic, and my thoughts went to Sid. Why had he sung my praises to Lois? Did I dare ask him?

I quickly made a right, escaping the congestion, and a few blocks later pulled into a convenience store parking lot. I got out of my car and entered the brightly lit store. Hot dogs roasting on a rotisserie held my attention for only a second. Two women waited for their order. A man was buying cigarettes at the counter. All had glanced up when I'd opened the door. The man nodded to me. I gave him a preoccupied smile, looked around for the pay phone, and spotted it next to a display of Budweiser beer.

I rummaged for change in my purse, saw the container of flower preservative, and sighed. If I didn't get rid of some of this stuff, I was going to become lopsided from hauling it around.

I deposited the coins, then dialed a number that I dislike using. A conversation with Sheriff Sid Hancock, more often than not, brought on a whopping headache, or at least that was his complaint. On my end, it wasn't my head that hurt but my ears. Sid has an annoying habit of sounding off in a very loud fashion. A telephone conversation about a topic I proposed to introduce would result in an assault on my hearing.

"Hancock, here," answered Sid, on the fourth ring.

"Hi. It's Bretta." Instinctively, I moved the phone three inches from my ear.

"What the hell do you want? Are you still in Branson? Why are you calling me?"

"Has Bailey Monroe contacted you lately?" It was a shot in the dark, but it zinged in, right on target. Sid sucked in his breath, then released it in a whoosh.

"Bretta," he began, but I interrupted him.

"What's going on, Sid? Why has a lid been put on the McDuffys' deaths?"

"Leave it alone, Bretta. This is out of your league. I sure the hell know it's out of mine. If you meddle in this, I'll be visiting you at Leavenworth."

I blinked. Leavenworth was a federal prison. Federal? I swallowed the uncomfortable lump that rose in my throat. "If I knew what was going on, Sid, I'd—"

I should've known it was coming, but I was too engrossed with what I was saying to move the phone away from my ear. Sid's next words burst through the receiver and reverberated in my brain.

"Damnit to hell, Bretta, you don't have to know everything. This doesn't concern you—"

"Not directly, but indirectly I've been dragged into it. Whatever 'it' might be. The McDuffys gave me an envelope to keep for them."

"Get rid of it! Get rid of it! Give it to—" His voice dwindled away.

"Yes?" I asked coolly. "Who should I give it to, Sid?"

"Listen, Bretta. Listen real carefully. Don't ask any questions. For once in your life, do as I say. Take that envelope to 708 Pine Tree Lane. Ask for Anthony, but that's the only inquiry you make. Got it?"

Slowly I hung up the phone. Yeah, I got it. 708 Pine Tree Lane. That was the address to the Eternal Rest Chapel. It looked like I had one more stop to make before going back to the hotel.

Five minutes later I parked my car in the same place Bailey had that morning. Shored up by a need to get to the bottom of whatever was going on, I brazenly moved to the back door of the chapel and tried the doorknob. It was unlocked. I ignored the neatly printed sign—PLEASE RING BEFORE ENTERING—that hung above the bell and walked in. I continued down a hall until I came to a door marked OFFICE.

Taking a deep breath, I squared my shoulders and stepped inside. My sudden appearance made the old man behind the desk sit up straight in his chair. He was dressed decorously in a dark suit and tie. His hair was gray, eyes solemn and direct.

"Oh," he said. "I didn't hear the front doorbell."

"I didn't come in the front door. I came around to the back."

"I see. My name is Anthony Bardova. How may I help you?"

"I've come to see the McDuffys."

Instantly he was alert, but his propriety never wavered. He flashed a smile, but his right hand dropped out of sight. "You have reason to believe they're here?"

"Bailey Monroe told me," I lied.

Anthony never took his eyes off mine. "Mr. Monroe is a friend of yours?"

"We're acquainted. May I see Mabel and Vincent, please?"

He pushed away from the desk, and I thought he was going to lead the way to the McDuffys, but he merely leaned back in his chair. "I don't believe I caught your name."

"That's because I never tossed it." He chuckled and crossed his legs, settling in for a pleasant visit. Softly, I asked, "Are you waiting for the next of kin to claim the bodies? Their daughter, Stephanie, died last month, so whom have you contacted?"

Finally, I'd shaken Anthony's composure. He uncrossed his legs and stood up. "I think you'd better go," he said, walking around his desk.

From the look in his eye, I knew he was about to politely escort me from the room and out of the chapel. In my present mood I wasn't willing to budge. Then like a typical female, I changed my mind. I smiled at Anthony and turned toward the door. He opened it, and we traded smiles, again.

I was facing the back door, where Anthony assumed I'd go. I played along, even took a step in that direction before pivoting on my toe and hotfooting it down the hall bound for the scenic route. I had a nice head start before the old man grasped my intention. I was randomly opening doors, peering in, and backing out when he caught up to me.

"Don't do that," he said, putting a hand on my arm. "Please. You can't—"

I shrugged him away and threw open another door. Since I was in a funeral home, I'd prepared myself for any and all situations, but never what I got. Bailey and another man were seated at a table covered with papers, a chrome cell phone, and a laptop computer. Neither man appeared surprised by my sudden entry. In fact, Bailey beckoned me into the room, then nodded to Anthony, who backed out and quietly closed the door.

Bailey shook his head. "I've had several informative chats with Sheriff Hancock, but he didn't do you justice. He told me you were clever and . . . uh . . . tenacious. I understand you're inquiring about the McDuffys."

At my amazed look, Bailey pointed to a speaker in the corner of the room. "When you mentioned their name, Anthony switched on the intercom. Sheriff Hancock called to tell us that you would be dropping off an envelope. You must have been in the area because Reggie and I weren't expecting you quite so soon."

Bailey glanced at my empty hands. "I don't see that envelope. Where is it, Bretta? I want it, and I want it now."

It was on the tip of my tongue to say that "People in hell want ice water," but I swallowed that comment and lied instead. "I don't have it with me."

Bailey traded glances with Reggie, who had shaggy brown hair and prominent eyes in a thin face. He wore grungy blue jeans, a black T-shirt with a torn pocket, and a pair of dirty sneakers.

"We could get a search warrant," said Reggie, "but I hesitate going to that extreme when we don't know what's in the envelope. It could be nothing, but then again—" He lifted a shoulder. "It'll have to be your call, Bailey. You're more familiar with the participants."

They leaned across the table, speaking in hushed tones. I looked from Bailey's spit and polish to Reggie's disheveled appearance. The latter looked like a thug, while Bailey gave the impression of impeccable respectability.

"Impression" was the tip-off that set my mind to whirling.

Who was Bailey trying to impress? Then it hit me like a wallop between the eyes. I'm no prodigy, but I'm not a fool. Even if Reggie were cleaned up, I'd never give him another thought. But Bailey had worked hard to catch my attention, and he'd done it superbly.

From the beginning, he'd let me know that we had many things in common. I felt a flash of betrayal when I remembered how he'd sympathized about Carl's death. I thought I'd found someone who understood my loneliness. But why had he singled me out? What did he hope to gain from making my acquaintance?

Apparently, Bailey hadn't known about the McDuffys' envelope until Sid told him a short time ago. So that wasn't it. Bailey had begun his observance of me before he'd gotten the call about the "bodies." If I followed this line of reasoning, whatever was going on had started before the McDuffys were murdered. Somehow I figured into this, but I wasn't sure how, unless it had to do with the florist convention.

I took a step forward. Reggie slammed the laptop shut, then shuffled the scattered papers. His actions briefly exposed a badge, lying on the table. I caught sight of a gold eagle and the words—"Department of Justice."

I ignored Reggie, concentrating on Bailey. He still had the ability to leave me giddy, but now for another reason. I'd stepped into the middle of a federal investigation. I wanted reassurance from Bailey. I wanted comfort. If he would've stood up and opened his arms, I'd have walked into his embrace without hesitation.

But this man, who sat at the table, was a different Bailey Monroe than the one who'd stroked my hand and kissed my lips. Had the attention he'd paid me been part of the investigation?

The two men were still whispering. I broke into their gabfest, directing a question at Bailey. "Why have you been hanging around me?"

"I'm not at liberty to answer *your* questions."

His abrupt tone hurt, but I kept my voice under control. "All right, then let me tell you a few facts. The McDuffys slid an envelope under the door of my room. In a note addressed to me, they requested that I keep the envelope for them until they came back for it. The note also advised that if they didn't return, I was to open the envelope and assess the contents."

Bailey listened closely. "Which you've done?"

"Yes, but only after I made numerous attempts to contact them. Since they didn't retrieve the envelope or make an effort to find me, I've put two and two together. The couple found at the bottom of the ravine was the McDuffys."

"Not bad," said Reggie. He smirked at Bailey. "I see what you mean about her."

I didn't appreciate the comment or the look he'd given Bailey, but I focused on what I wanted to say. "You went out of your way to meet me in the hotel. Why? What did you expect me to tell you? What did you want from me?"

Bailey fielded my questions with questions. "Why wouldn't I look to you for insight when you possess a plethora of knowledge? By your own admission you're capable of putting two and two together. How do we know you haven't used your expertise for less than honorable reasons? How do we know you found the envelope in your room? Perhaps you stole it from the McDuffys. Why wouldn't you become a suspect in the McDuffys' double homicide?"

The words "suspect" and "double homicide" blew what little composure I had left. When I'd recovered enough air so I could speak, I said, "The envelope held a picture of their daughter, Stephanie, a cassette tape, and a note to me. None of which are motives for me to commit murder."

"So you say," said Bailey. "But now that the envelope has been opened, how are we to know you didn't privately remove a piece of incriminating evidence?"

"Because I'm telling you I did not."

Bailey shrugged. "Just your being here is suspicious. Weren't you told this afternoon by a Branson police officer not to leave the hotel?"

"Yes, but he said if I did leave, I had to tell the people at the front desk where I was going."

"So they know you're here?"

I swallowed. "No. I said I was taking a drive." The quick glance Bailey shot Reggie made my hands shake. "You aren't going to tell me anything, are you?"

Both men stared. I could have told them that it was in their best interests to have me as an ally, rather than blunder on my own, but I didn't. I left the room, pulling the door shut. Before the latch caught, I heard Reggie say, "Maybe we should've taken her into custody."

Bailey replied, "I'll keep an eye on her."

His brusque tone, more than Reggie's suggestion, brought tears to my eyes, but I blinked them away. Anthony hadn't put in an appearance, so I let myself out the back door of the funeral chapel.

Before getting into my car, I stared up at the star-spangled sky. A short time ago I'd compared my perception of this investigation to a flower garden that had too many weeds. My analogy would have to be stretched to a grander scale. This was no longer a piddling backyard plot of tilled soil. I'd wandered smack dab into the middle of a national forest, and my "weeds" were more intimidating than I'd thought.

Chapter Sixteen

I walked into the hotel lobby and immediately thought I'd entered a one-man show. Hooked to a wireless microphone, Tyrone was addressing the floral conference attendees, who were ringed around the balconies. I glanced at my watch. There was less than forty minutes until the Mel Tillis show.

Alvin noted my arrival and sidled over. "Your association's president decided to speak from the lobby, rather than call for a group meeting in an appropriate area. I was given ten minutes to bring this assemblage out of their rooms." He nodded to the numerous spectators. "I've counted one hundred and eighty-seven, which isn't a bad turnout, if I do say so." He grimaced. "Not that I had a choice. Your president is a . . . uh . . . forceful man. He really gets off being the master of ceremonies."

"Ruler," I said. "Effie was right about the meaning of Tyrone's name. It suits him." Seeing Alvin's blank look, I pointed to Effie. "She's made it a hobby knowing the origin of names and their definitions, and how they relate to our personalities."

"That's interesting. I wonder what my name means." He raised an eyebrow. "Got any idea?"

"You'll have to ask Effie," I said, moving down a ramp to the older woman's side. "What have I missed?" I whispered.

She shook her head wearily. "Three tawdry jokes, dear."

173

I tuned in to Tyrone. "—asked you to gather here before leaving for this evening's festivities. My fellow florists, there has been an unfortunate accident. It isn't necessary for me to go into the particulars, but suffice it to say we've lost a valuable member of our association, as well as a good friend. Angelica Weston died this afternoon; however, the conference will go on as planned."

"When was this decision made?" I asked Effie.

"About an hour ago, against the board's unanimous vote."

"—no reason for us to give up our weekend. Gellie was full of fun and laughter. I'm sure she would've wanted us to carry on with our plans and make the most of this unfortunate situation."

"If that man says 'unfortunate' one more time I'm going to bust him," I muttered.

Effie patted my arm. "He's an ignoramus, and most of these people know it or if they didn't, they do now."

"In Angelica's honor, I've requested the hotel provide an 'Angelic' dessert for those of you who'd like to congregate in the east ballroom after the show this evening. I think it fitting that we share a period of reflection for our departed colleague."

Effie clicked her tongue disapprovingly. "The man has no concept of good taste."

I was steamed. The nerve. The absolute gall. To use *food* to celebrate Gellie's memory was the cruelest notion Tyrone could have hatched.

Tyrone continued, "Delia hurt her hand. Just this afternoon, Darren had to leave on an important assignment. This conference shall remain a fond memory for years to come, but I see no need to continue with the contest."

His announcement brought a hue and cry from the attendees. I gritted my teeth. If the conference was to go on as planned then so should the contest. I moved toward Tyrone with the intention of pointing this out.

Once I left the sidelines and entered his realm of limelight, the crowd applauded my arrival. Tyrone had his back to me. The microphone dangled from his hand. Before he knew what was happening, I snatched the apparatus and shouted, "Welcome to the first annual Show-Me-Floral Designers' Conference *AND CONTEST*."

My words brought bedlam to the balconies and twisted Tyrone's facial features into a savage fury. I quickly waved for silence. "I regret beginning our conference by disputing our esteemed president's decision, but the last time I checked, *I* was coordinator of the floral contest."

As I spoke into the microphone, my gaze circled the lobby. Chloe was dabbing her eyes. Robbee's hard stare was telepathic, willing me to name him as a new contestant. Bernice twitched with fury, while Allison didn't seem at all surprised by my actions. Back in the farthest corner near the café was Hubert, Darren's right-hand man. Why hadn't he left the hotel with his employer? Where was Miriam? I caught sight of her sitting at a table on the terrace lounge. When our eyes locked, she slowly nodded, then looked across the lobby to Hubert. Her head swiveled back to me, then back to him. What was she trying to tell me?

There wasn't time to figure it out now. I had one hundred and eighty-seven pairs of eyes drilling me. "As contest coordinator, it's my pleasure to announce that the contest—"

The microphone went dead. I turned and saw Tyrone had disconnected the battery pack that hung from the waistband of his trousers. I appealed to Alvin for assistance. He held up his hands helplessly. Tyrone's satisfied smile was premature. I would not be thwarted.

My country heritage rose from the depths of my diaphragm. In my younger days, when I'd lived on a farm, I'd been able to call the cows to the barn from a field that was a quarter of a mile away.

Graze. Green. I closed my eyes in order to concentrate, but someone yelled, "Come on, Bretta." I opened my eyes and shook my head to clear it. Cupping my hands to my lips, I cut loose. "CONTEST TEN O'CLOCK TOMORROW. BE THERE!"

I shoved the useless microphone into Tyrone's hand, turned on my heel, and stalked away amid cheers that threatened to bring the hotel down around our ears.

I made for Effie, who I knew I could count on for uncensured support. She welcomed me into the circle of her arms, and I rested my chin on her lavender curls. People underestimate the power of a hug. It was wonderful to be wrapped in an embrace and held close as if I truly mattered. Tears welled in my eyes, and I had to step away from the little woman before I blubbered all over her.

I patted her wrinkled cheek. "Thanks for standing by me."

Effie grimaced. "Of course I'll stand by you, dear, but I never should have *stood* by and let you provoke Tyrone. Rulers don't like to be embarrassed or defied."

I put my arm across her stooped shoulders. "Don't give it another thought. You couldn't have stopped me. Tyrone's insincerity regarding Gellie's death was more than I could take. Add in the fact that he canceled the contest, and my composure crumbled like a piece of overcooked bacon."

Effie peered up at me. "You must be hungry, dear."

I took stock of my physical condition—heart rate above normal, stomach gnawing for attention. "Yeah, I could use a bite." I looked up at the balconies. Most of the spectators were gone, but a few lingered, talking and laughing. Tyrone had vanished into his suite. Chloe and Robbee were leaving for the concert. As he passed through the doorway, Robbee glanced back at me and mouthed one word, "Please."

Hubert had disappeared, but Miriam was still on the terrace lounge. When our eyes met, she gestured to the chair opposite her.

Did I have the stamina to deal with her? My feet hurt, and my stomach demanded food. I sighed. A conversation with Miriam wouldn't last long. I'd either tick her off or she'd rile me, and that would be the end of it.

Beside me, Effie said, "I've been thinking, dear."

"What about?"

"Murder."

I took her arm and gently led her to a secluded corner. "But you've just been thinking about it, right?"

She chuckled. "While Tyrone was speaking, it was tempting, but I haven't done the deed."

"I meant you haven't been nosing around?"

"Just a smidgen."

My throat closed so I could barely get the words out. "Such as?"

"It seemed like it might be advantageous if I let everyone know that you're on the case. You know, shift the rock so to speak, then, like you said, our guilty party can slither out of hiding."

"Oh, my God."

"I think it will work, dear. I've seen it done on television, though we'll be smarter than those actors. We'll be on our toes, ready to nab the scoundrel."

I gazed into her faded blue eyes and spoke firmly. "Effie, you have to promise me that you'll go up to your room." I pictured the blood from the cut on Delia's hand, and quickly added, "Check your door handle before you touch it. Someone is playing a nasty game with razor blades."

"Razor blades?" Bewildered, she shook her head. "I don't understand. What kind of game could you play with something so menacing?"

For her own safety, I quickly filled her in on how Delia had been hurt. When I was finished the little woman was as pale as the white hankie she'd taken from her pocket. She dabbed her eyes.

"Someone is after you, dear? I won't have that, you know."

"I'll be fine, but I'm worried about you. Check your door, then go inside and lock up tight. I'll meet you in the contest room in the morning about seven. Okay?"

She looked as if she might argue before she turned and wobbled away. I watched her as she entered the elevator. I kept an eye on her when she got off at the third floor, and by taking several steps back, I could keep her in sight as she went to her door. She leaned close, inspected the lever, and then disappeared into her room.

I turned toward Miriam, hoping she'd given up and had left. Nope. She was still waiting. My shoulders drooped as I shuffled down the ramp to her table. It didn't enhance my mood to see her looking immaculate—every red hair in place, aquamarine-colored dress crisp and fresh, her makeup flawless. I wore the same pair of jeans and rose-pink sweater I'd put on this morning. I was sure my nose was shiny, my eyeliner smeared, and my lips as bloodless as a turnip. Suppressing the urge to sniff my armpits, I sat down and faced her with all the confidence I could muster.

"We could postpone this until later," I said. "If you plan on making the concert."

"I'm not going, but this won't take long." She looked over my shoulder.

I turned, and a waiter smiled politely. "May I get you ladies something?"

I seized the opportunity. "Have room service deliver a grilled chicken salad and a diet Coke to 521. I'll be there shortly." The waiter nodded, then looked at Miriam, who waved him impatiently away.

"Okay," I said, "let's get this over. You've got something on your mind, and I'm too tired and too hungry to play psychic. You wanted me to see Hubert, and I took note. Somehow you got rid of Darren. What difference does it make if Hubert hangs around?"

Miriam's green eyes narrowed. "Your attitude is the very reason why I didn't come to you in the first place. There was no way you'd listen to what I had to say." She scooted her chair away from the table. "You aren't the only one to question what's going on. I've been suspicious for a year, but it wasn't until I got to know Delia at the semifinals that I finally put it all together."

I waved my hand in a circular motion. "What?"

"All I wanted was to keep this contest fair and aboveboard for everyone. Delia was adamant at making you reveal the categories. I never wanted them disclosed because I wanted to see Darren's repertoire of designs."

Abruptly she stood up. "When I found out that Tyrone was considering appointing Darren as a one-man show and giving the rest of us token awards, I slapped his face. But what you did this evening was much more debilitating. Thank you for overriding his decision to cancel the contest." Her mouth split with a spiteful grin. "That was a marvelous show. I'd pay twice the price to see it again."

As I watched Miriam walk away, I murmured, "Reper-toire." That peculiar word had stuck in my brain since I'd heard Darren use it.

I headed for my room using the elevator. If someone had told me two days ago that I'd feel safe in the glass box, where I was plainly visible, I'd have thought they were nuts. There hadn't been any more razor-blade episodes, but I wasn't taking chances. I had two empty boxes in my purse. The missing blades were like miniature guillotines hanging over my head.

On the ride up to the fifth floor, I wondered what kind of public denouncement Miriam had hoped to hear. It must have something to do with Darren. Gellie had said that he had come to the semifinals prepared with glamellia blossoms fabri-cated from gladiolus florets. While Darren's clever gimmick wasn't proper, it was hardly worth pitching a fit over. It had been Gellie who'd brought the contrived flowers to the judges' attention when Miriam had refused to get involved. And yet for the last two days, Miriam had conspired "to keep the con-test fair and aboveboard for everyone."

Contrived—conspired—repertoire. The three words formed a picture I didn't like, but that didn't mean I was right. When the elevator had deposited me on my floor, I saw Hubert waiting in the hall outside my room. In his hand was a perfect peach rose with a bow and card attached.

He saw me and smiled shyly. "I promised I'd personally deliver this to you, Mrs. Solomon." He thrust the flower into my hand and turned to leave.

"Please wait," I said. "I assume this is from Darren?" When the old man nodded, I indicated my room. "Come on in while I read the card. I may want to reply."

I checked the handle, unlocked the door, and flipped on the

lights. Reluctantly, Hubert followed me. "Have a seat," I invited, gesturing to the chairs by the window.

He crossed the room and perched on the edge of a cushion. His black slacks were neatly creased, his shirt an ebony silk. As I nudged my suitcase aside, an apple rolled across the bottom. I stared at it before I sat on the bed and read the card. It simply stated that Darren was sorry, followed by his name signed in a tight scrawl at the bottom.

"Darren hopes you'll understand," said Hubert.

Slowly, I nodded. "Yeah. It's coming to me, but not what Darren might have expected." I laid the rose and card on the nightstand. "I was present when he won his first competition." Reaching into the open suitcase, I picked up the red apple. "This is a Jonathan, and Darren used Granny Smith, but the end result would be the same."

I smiled and tossed the apple to Hubert, who caught it easily. "I've always remembered those apples Darren carved into swans. Show me how it's done, Hubert."

"I really don't know—"

"Oh, yes, you do. Aren't you tired of the deception?"

Instead of answering, Hubert pulled a red-handled knife from his pocket. His hand shook ever so slightly as he worked the blade from its casing. "My grandfather was a whittler— bars of soap, pieces of fruit—but not a wood-carver. He thought that sounded too grand for an idle hobby. When he held a knife, he drew a crowd, reveling in the attention, telling stories about the creation he was shaping. I was five when he gave me my first cutting tool." The stainless-steel blade sliced through the crisp apple. "The minute I grasped that knife in my grubby little hand images were in my brain, and my fingers know exactly what to do."

Darren had said those same words to Miriam, but in his case they'd sounded pretentious. Hubert was stating a fact. "And you taught Darren?" I asked.

"It took days. I had to trace each cutting line with a Magic Marker before he got the hang of it." Three more times Hubert cut into the apple. "It isn't difficult if you can visualize, but that's Darren's problem. He can copy, but he doesn't have imagination. I make the original designs, he memorizes them down to the placement of a single piece of greenery."

"But he does his arrangements with such finesse. How is that possible?"

"If you do something long enough it becomes second nature." Hubert bent over the apple. "Just a couple more cuts—"

"Why wasn't he apprehensive about this contest? With the categories kept a secret wasn't he worried about making a good showing?"

Hubert didn't answer right away. He dipped the point of his knife into the apple and gave it a couple of twists. After wiping his creation with a handkerchief he'd taken from his pocket, he presented a swan to me, nestled in the palm of his hand. I admired his work, then placed it next to the rose on the nightstand.

"The categories didn't matter to Darren," said Hubert, cleaning the blade of his knife and putting it back in his pocket. "He's learned a number of designs that would fit any occasion. You could have said, 'Night of the Black Moon,' and I would bet he'd have reached for a low container. Next would have been a white football mum, standing tall and straight, with a cluster of the darkest purple flowers at the base. He'd have joked with the audience, whipping his knife accurately through the flower stems. When he was finished with his creation, he'd have presented his bouquet with aplomb, making you gasp with admiration."

"And you've seen him complete this design?"

Hubert scoffed. "Seen him? I created it for the France design symposium that was held last year. Darren taught one hundred and forty florists that more isn't necessarily best." He smirked. "Regardless of what Martha Stewart says."

"How could you allow him to take credit for your creativity?"

Hubert shrugged. "My job at Delia's shop was going nowhere. She reserved all the specialty orders for herself, leaving me the bud vases, mugs, or simple hospital and sympathy arrangements. When she was away on vacation, I learned that I had a knack for making a more dramatic showing. Darren came to work for her and expressed a desire to learn."

Sadly, he shook his head. "She teased him about being a budding artiste—at driving a delivery van—and dared him to enter that contest. He and I got along well. I had the inventiveness, and he had the personality to carry it off. Teaming up with Darren was the best thing that could have happened to me."

Hubert sat staring off into space and a smile touched his lips. "You asked if I was tired of the deception?" Before I could answer, he shifted his gaze to the carving on the nightstand. "I might not have been the swan, Mrs. Solomon, but at least I got to swim on the lake."

Chapter Seventeen

The arrival of my salad was the excuse that sent Hubert on his way. I picked at the food, took a shower, and then climbed into bed. My body craved rest, but my mind wouldn't stop spinning. I was furious with Darren for having conned the industry I loved, but it was Hubert's last comment that kept me tossing and turning.

"I might not have been the swan, but at least I got to swim on the lake."

It was a picturesque way of saying that he hadn't been the star of the show, but he'd had a supporting role and was important in the overall scheme of things. Wasn't that the way I felt when I got caught up in a case? By finding the truth, I was making a difference in someone's life, while at the same time, my involvement helped me believe that I still mattered.

I flopped over on my stomach and bunched the pillow under my head. This wasn't the best time to analyze my past, if I wanted to go to sleep. But I couldn't stop my thoughts.

Before Carl died, I'd seen myself as an independent businesswoman. And in that area, I had been self-reliant and confident. What I hadn't counted on was how Carl's love had shaped the rest of my life. Once he was gone, I'd faced a major upheaval in everything around me—everything except my flower shop, but then, he'd never been involved with that aspect of my life.

I'd searched for ways to ease the pain I'd felt at his passing. I'd sold the home he and I had shared and bought the mansion that was more ostentatious than anything I'd ever dreamed of owning. I'd changed my physical appearance to the point that when I looked in the mirror it was as if I were seeing another woman.

My mother had believed that a well-centered person didn't manipulate life's circumstances but made the best of any given situation. Effie had offered the same advice, but with a twist another florist could appreciate—bloom where you're planted.

When I looked at my history from this perspective, it would seem I was a fantastic manipulator. Instead of blooming where I was planted, I'd eased my roots from my own flowerbed and transplanted them elsewhere, hoping to claim a piece of someone else's life as a means of rounding out my own.

Snuggling deeper under the covers, I closed my eyes and forced myself to lie still. There have been times when my bouts of sleeplessness have brought discovery. Some of my best plans were made at night while the rest of the world snoozed. However, at this particular moment, lying in a strange bed, away from home and all that was familiar, I was at a loss.

I was tired. Tired of thinking. Tired of swimming alone on the lake. I sighed and ran my fingers over the cold sheets at my side. Mostly, I was tired of sleeping alone. Maybe that's how Gellie and Stephanie had felt, too. At age fifty, Gellie had undergone major surgery to help her lose weight. Stephanie's picture had showed a young woman desperate to have a life. After coming home from Branson she'd been filled with hopes and dreams.

Graze—eat. Weight—gain. Starve—die.

I squeezed my eyes shut. It was there. The thought was just an embryo. If I could relax, my subconscious might make it flourish.

I was dozing restlessly when there was a knock on my door. I burrowed deeper under the covers, but the tapping became insistent. I flipped on the lamp and looked at the clock. It was after 1:00 A.M.

"Who is it?" I called.

"Bretta, it's Robbee. I have to talk to you."

"Not now."

"It's about Stephanie."

That brought me wide-awake. I rubbed my eyes and creaked out of bed. "Wait a second," I called as I put on my robe. After a brief visit to the bathroom, I unlatched the door. "This better be good," I said. He was dressed in evening clothes, minus his tie. The first three buttons of his shirt were undone. "Damned good," I muttered as he walked past me, wafting the aroma of liquor. I shut the door and faced him. "I hope this isn't a drunken plea for me to okay you as a contestant."

"I'm not drunk. I had a couple glasses of wine."

I motioned to the chair Hubert had occupied earlier, then watched Robbee closely to see if he staggered. He seemed in control of his faculties. I sat on my bed and pulled a blanket around my shoulders. "What about Stephanie?"

"You asked me if I mailed her presents or letters?" I nodded. "Not once did I send her anything. I could have taken advantage of her, but I didn't. She was nice, Bretta. I wouldn't have set her up to be hurt."

"But that didn't stop you from spreading on the charm. You might not have meant for her to read more into your actions, but I think she did. And you *know* she did. That's what brought you here tonight. You feel guilty, and you want me to assure you that everything is fine."

I tossed off the blanket and stood up. "I won't do that. Stephanie is the one you owe an explanation to, but she's dead." Robbee winced. I steadily surveyed him. "Her parents are dead, too."

Robbee's forehead creased with a frown. "Stephanie told me her mother had cancer, but what happened to her father?"

"They were murdered."

Robbee's eyes widened, and he jerked upright in his chair. "Murdered?" he repeated. "When? Where?"

"I don't know the particulars," I said, "but an investigation is quietly taking place here in Branson. I want your word that this information won't go any further than this room. Which means no florist grapevine."

Robbee slowly nodded. "Last fall I called the McDuffys' house to talk Stephanie into selling me some of her pictures, but she was too sick to come to the phone. Mabel told me that Stephanie hadn't been ill until she came back from Branson. I commented that Stephanie might have picked up a flu bug; Mabel was convinced her daughter's illness was more serious, but she couldn't persuade her to go to the doctor. She said Stephanie had trouble breathing, was depressed, and wouldn't eat. She just sipped tea—"

"—listened to music, and watched for the mail," I finished softly. I sat down on the bed and pulled the blanket around my shoulders. "Gellie drank tea, too," I said aloud. "She even carried her own tea bags."

"What does Gellie's . . . uh . . . death have to do with Stephanie's or her parents?"

"I haven't figured out every detail, but Stephanie visits

Branson, then goes home, where she gets sick and dies. Her parents come to Branson, and they're murdered. Gellie arrives in Branson a day ahead of what she tells us. She met with someone who she said had approached her with an idea last year, and two days later she's dead."

"When you put it that way, it does seem suspicious, but who or what connects it?"

Now was my chance. I stared him in the eye. "Is it you?"

"Me?" He licked his lips and tried to smile, but it was a feeble effort. "I'm not a killer, Bretta. I may have a hundred character flaws, but murderous intent isn't one of them."

"If you're lying, Robbee, kill me now, because I'm going to figure this out."

A spark of the old razzle-dazzle shone in his eyes. "I'm in your bedroom, and you're dressed in a flimsy robe. Killing you isn't my first impulse."

I pulled the blanket tighter around my shoulders and gave him a disgusted glare. "I didn't think it was you, but I had to ask. Did you happen to notice who's on duty at the front desk?"

"Ruby. Why?"

"Darn. I wish Helen were here." I frowned at Robbee. "You and this Ruby are on a first-name basis?"

Robbee's tone was defensive. "What's wrong with that?"

"Go down there and see if you can talk her into giving you the key to the McDuffys' room."

"Good Lord, Bretta, you aren't asking for much. How in the world am I going to do that? What kind of excuse can I use?" His eyes narrowed. "Besides, if the McDuffys have been murdered, won't their room be sealed?"

"Nothing's been officially announced. I think the 'powers that be' are waiting to see what develops."

"But if we're caught in that room—"

We haggled for another fifteen minutes, but in the end, I had my way. Shame and guilt were mighty weapons, and I used both barrels. Robbee was scowling when he left, but I had no doubt that he'd wile his way around Ruby to get what I wanted.

I used the time he was gone to get dressed and to flesh out my plan. It stood to reason that with the murder of the McDuffys, they'd found the person who'd led their daughter astray. To do that they must've had more information than what they'd shared with me. Bailey would have gone over the room. I wanted that chance, too.

I waited for Robbee, wavering between going on with my plan or going back to bed. I stomped around the room, irritated with myself. I was doing it again. Getting involved in something that wasn't any of my business, and yet, how could I turn my back on Vincent and Mabel's final plea for justice?

Effie had said that I might have a God-given talent for helping others. Carl had thought I had potential or he'd never have taken the time to educate me. Just as my eyes were blue and my hair was brown, I finally admitted that this was to be my lot in life. I wasn't going to change—even for a federal investigation.

When the knock sounded on my door, my shoulders were squared. I opened the door to find Effie standing in the hall. My eyes nearly popped out of their sockets.

I took her arm and hurried her inside, where I gave her the once-over. She looked okay—no blood, no cuts, and no tears. But I was suspicious of the blush that stained her wrinkled cheeks. My gaze traveled from her polyester pantsuit to her soft-soled slippers.

"Effie, what are you doing still dressed? I hope you haven't been snooping around the hotel?"

"I can't do a surveillance of the entire building, so I took the stairs to the lobby and hid behind a plant near the front door. It was a good spot, dear. I was able to observe the comings and goings of everyone. I had quite an adventure. Of course, the man that does maintenance on the tropical plants won't ever be the same." She tittered at the memory.

It made me crazy with worry to think about her going up and down that stairwell. I could have given her chapter and verse about the dangers involved in snooping, but I knew my warning would fall on deaf ears. So I tried another tact. "Effie, you need your rest. Everyone's asleep by now, probably even our killer."

"We can only surmise what the killer is doing, dear, and everyone is not asleep. I saw Robbee flirting with the front desk clerk. When I heard him mention the McDuffys' name, I came up here to tell you."

Before I could answer there was a knock on the door. Effie's eyes widened when I let Robbee into my room. His face was flushed; his hand shook as he held up the plastic key.

"Got it," he said unnecessarily. "But it cost the association two dozen red roses, arranged and delivered to Ruby before she goes off duty at six A.M."

"That's all it took?"

He made a face. "Her boyfriend won't propose. Ruby hopes when he sees the bouquet that has come from a 'secret admirer,' he'll pop the question." Robbee glared at me. "Don't ever shame me again, Bretta. Women are just as manipulative as any man could ever be." He glanced around and saw Effie. "This is a pleasant surprise—I think."

"Effie was just on her way to her room. We'll escort her before we go upstairs."

"Upstairs?" said Effie. "What door does that key unlock?"

I briefly sketched out my plan and promised to fill her in tomorrow on what I'd found in the McDuffys' room. She wasn't interested in a replay. She wanted firsthand knowledge. I knew I was in trouble when she crossed her arms over her shrunken bosom and tapped her slipper stubbornly.

I tried one more time. "If the three of us traipse upstairs someone is sure to wonder what's going on."

Effie nodded to Robbee. "Leave him here." She got this devious gleam in her eye. "Or perhaps you'd like me to go back to my lookout in the lobby?"

Well, hell no. I sure didn't want that. "Fine, fine. Let's get on with this. What's the room number?"

Robbee said, "One floor up—609."

I took a deep breath to steady my nerves and opened the door. Peering along my balcony and those across the way, I beckoned for my dynamic duo to follow me. In the stairwell, I tried to take Effie's arm, but she shrugged off my help. The little woman was testy, out to prove a point. I kept the lead up to the next floor and down the hall to room 609. Behind me, Robbee hummed nervously.

"Stop making that annoying sound," I whispered as I fit the plastic key in the slot. The tiny lights flashed from red to green. Taking another deep breath, I pushed open the door, grabbed Effie's arm, and hustled her into the room with me. Robbee was right on our heels.

Once the door was closed, I flipped on the lights. I held that gulp of oxygen until I'd focused on a normal hotel room, with normal furnishings, then the pent-up air swooshed out in a sigh of relief.

"Both of you stay here," I said softly. "I'll take a quick look, then we're gone."

Robbee had his back plastered against the door. His wide-eyed gaze darted around the room. "I don't see anything," he said. "Do you?"

"Give me a minute."

Effie whispered, "What are you looking for, dear?"

"I'm not sure."

This room had the same layout as mine—bath/dressing rooms on my left, bedroom straight ahead. I noted that the closet door was ajar, but the open suitcase on the bed drew me forward.

I knew better than to manhandle the garments in the suitcase, but I shifted them ever so slightly to see what was underneath. The dusty cuff of a pair of Vincent's trousers gave me pause. I dug deeper and discovered what I took to be a blouse of Mabel's with a splotch of something yellow—mustard?—on the front. That stained blouse was neatly folded with three others—all fleshly laundered. Vincent's dirty pants were mixed in with his clean clothes.

Why put the soiled clothes in with the clean clothes? Only a real slob would do that, and that was hardly my impression of the McDuffys. But if the contents of this room had been tossed in a frantic effort to locate something incriminating, perhaps the killer might have second thoughts in leaving it obviously searched. Would that person have taken the time to fold each garment back into the suitcase, inadvertently mixing the dirty clothes with the clean? A glance in the room by a maid wouldn't have raised any alarms if everything were neat and tidy.

"Look on the armoire," said Robbee quietly.

I did as directed and saw a framed picture of pressed flowers. In this picture, Stephanie had abandoned Monet's impressionist style to construct a visual image of this hotel with Haversham Hall and the conservatory dome in the distance.

Snippets of leaves, minute twigs, fragile blossoms, delicate seeds, and an inventive mind had blended nature's bounty into a marvel. In the foreground was a replica of the tour bus that was no bigger than a postage stamp. I studied it closely and saw itsy-bitsy people waiting in line to get on board.

Mesmerized, I picked the picture up. Stephanie must have used tweezers to set each particle into place. Since Robbee had already told me who'd been on the tour, I was able to put a name to the figures. Like a caricaturist, Stephanie had parodied each. A rounded shape made by a watermelon seed made me wonder if it represented the artist. I nodded when I saw that behind her was a figure sporting a diminutive ponytail fashioned from what looked like dried corn silks.

Corn? I smirked. Maybe Stephanie hadn't been so infatuated with Robbee that she couldn't see him for what he was. Red petals represented Miriam's hair. Zach's muscles were minuscule pods. Tyrone wore a crown of iridescent feathers. Peacock, I decided. I assumed the shape behind Tyrone was Bernice, who was linked to our esteemed president by a chain made of prickly sand burrs. Darren's head was out of proportion to the rest of his body. I interpreted it to mean that he was egotistical and full of himself.

Stephanie must have liked Gellie. She'd portrayed the equally heavy woman with grace. Her flowing gown was made of golden sunflower petals. Looking closely I saw Gellie was holding a cluster of tiny green leaves. The last cartoon I guessed to be Alvin. His pale skin had been fabricated from the husk of an onion, and he seemed to be urging everyone toward the tour bus.

"The McDuffys brought this picture with them for a reason," I said. "Something about it must have been a clue to them as to who they were looking for. I wonder if Stephanie talked about each figure as she created it, naming them, and relating personal details?"

"May I see it, dear?"

I handed the frame to Effie. She brought her nose to within four inches of the glass, examining each particle. Twice she chuckled. Once she sucked in her breath, as if amazed or surprised.

"What is it?" I asked.

"Just an impression, dear. Stephanie could have been a psychologist. She's captured the essence of each of our colleagues' personalities. While I find names fascinating, this young woman has delved deeper into the psyche of each individual. And if I understand the facts correctly, she did this analysis in a single afternoon?"

When I nodded, Effie sighed softly. "That in itself is impressive, while at the same time it's also upsetting."

"How's that?" asked Robbee, peeking over Effie's shoulder. "It's just a picture. I don't see why you'd call it upsetting."

"I understand what Effie means," I said quietly. "If Stephanie could pinpoint each person's character so accurately, then how was she 'led astray'?"

Effie beamed at me. "That's right, dear. It would seem that Stephanie had intellect and intuitiveness, but she must have had an Achilles' heel. She was vulnerable in some area of her life, and if we're to figure this out, we have to make that discovery."

Softly, I put my thoughts into words. "It was her weight. Gellie, too. Both women were desperate to have a normal life. In the Topiary Cotillion, Gellie told me that 'our extra pounds tethered us to this earth.' Lavelle had described Stephanie's mood when she returned from Branson as being 'higher than a kite' because she'd met a man. I let the cliché slip past me,

194

accepting Lavelle's explanation because I didn't know Stephanie personally. However, I knew Gellie very well. She wasn't herself in the lobby, and when she danced in the Topiary Cotillion, she was out of control. She was—higher than a kite."

Effie studied me. "Do you think they were taking drugs?"

"It makes sense. The McDuffys said in their note that Stephanie had changed. Being hooked on drugs alters a person's personality and their life. Stephanie watched for the mail. I thought she was a lovesick woman, but what if she'd been waiting for her next drug delivery? Gellie's behavior was extreme. She laughed and smiled, yet there were moments of despair when she gave in to tears." My voice was grim. "But it was her actions before she died that should've alerted me."

Wearily, I leaned my head against the armoire. A drug abuser's family is often the last to recognize that there's a problem. I wasn't Gellie's family, but I was her friend.

My lips curled at the word. This person called "Friend" had doled out illegal drugs, preyed on women after their trust was won, and murdered innocent people. All in the guise of being a friend.

We weren't dealing with an ordinary weed in my garden design. This species was as vile and noxious as poison ivy and just as invasive.

Chapter Eighteen

"Bretta?" said Robbee.

His tone jerked me out of my thoughts. "Okay. Let's go before we get caught."

"Too late for that, dear," said Effie. She nodded to the closet door that was standing open. "We have company."

I followed her gaze and saw Bailey step into the room. Perspiration glistened on his forehead. Damp circles under his arms indicated that he was more than hot under the collar.

My heart was clattering like a four-cylinder engine in a full-sized truck. I was scared, but I tried to hide it under a false sense of bravado. "It must have been uncomfortable in there," I said, nodding to the closet. "Good thing you don't have a phobia like . . . let me see. Was that your second wife or was it the third?"

Bailey took a step toward me. "Woman, you are in serious trouble."

"I don't see why. We have a key. Robbee, show him." Like a puppet his arm snapped up displaying the piece of plastic. "See," I said. "No unlawful entry. Ruby, at the front desk, agreed it might be a good idea if we checked on the McDuffys. As I'm sure you're aware, no one here at the hotel has been informed that the couple won't be coming back."

"But you knew. This room is part of an ongoing investigation."

Robbee spun to the door, clawing at the latch. Bailey was at his side in two strides and put a hand on the wooden panel. "No one is going anywhere," he said. "If you don't think I have the authority or 'just cause' to haul your interfering hides off to jail, then keep right on talking."

I opened my mouth but couldn't get a word out. Satisfied, Bailey nodded. "Now we're getting somewhere. Just for the record, I'm Special Agent Bailey Monroe." He reached into his pocket and displayed his badge.

"See, dear, I was right. Your Mr. Bailey is law enforcement." Effie smiled coyly up at Bailey. "Your name has an Old French origin. I'd say from the moment of conception, you were destined to be a policeman. I assume your father is, also?"

Bailey blinked. "Pop was an elementary school teacher."

Effie's face crumpled with disappointment. Bailey stared at her. He stared at me. From the way his expression changed, he'd reached the conclusion that I was the obvious target for his frustration. "You, Ms. Solomon, have dibbled and dabbled in *my* investigation. I want your cooperation, but I also want you to butt out for your own safety and mine."

"How in the world have I caused you any problems?"

"Let's begin with your reason for being in here. What were you looking for?"

"Nothing specific," I admitted. "I've never met the McDuffys, but they trusted me with the envelope. I never met Stephanie, their daughter who passed away last month, but her death has set off a chain of events that has drawn me in."

"Such as?" prompted Bailey.

I averted my gaze to the carpet. Bailey had every right to hear the facts, but did he have the right to my speculations? And what if I told him what I was thinking? What if I was way off base? Or worse. What if he laughed at me?

"Will you answer one question?" I asked.

"I have to hear it first."

"What agency are you with?"

"I'm DEA—Drug Enforcement Agency."

A combination of fatigue, stress, and being right about something that was so wrong made my knees buckle. I pitched against the armoire, jarring Stephanie's picture. When it toppled, I grabbed the wooden frame to keep it from hitting the floor.

I glanced at Bailey. "Stephanie and Gellie were both taking something. You were already investigating that when the McDuffys were murdered. You're here to find the pusher—the distributor?"

"Have I found her?" asked Bailey smoothly.

At first I didn't grasp his meaning. When his words finally sunk in, I clenched my jaw. We stared at each other, and after a moment I relaxed enough to ask, "Do you always wear Old Spice cologne or was that part of your cover?"

Bailey almost smiled—almost—but not quite. "When I'm on a case I use every advantage I can get. Once I informed Sheriff Hancock that I needed personal information about you and those close to you, he came through. You have a keen mind, Bretta, but that's inherent in a shrewd criminal. It's always the least suspected that proves to be the hardest to catch."

"My God, Bailey, when you accused me of being a suspect in the McDuffys' murder, I thought you were baiting me so I'd blurt out information. Now you're accusing me of being the mastermind of a drug ring? I'm not Sid's favorite person, but he would never tell you that I have criminal tendencies."

Bailey replied, "Khat."

I raised my eyebrows. "Is that supposed to mean something to me?"

He reeled off a bunch of words. "Khat. K-h-a-t. African salad. *Catha edulis*. Cat. Chat. Quat. Abyssinian tea. African tea. Take your pick."

"Tea?" I repeated.

"Uh-oh," said Robbee, looking at me in disbelief. "You were right to suspect the tea."

Bailey swung his gaze to Robbee. "What are you talking about?"

"Bretta had made the connection that both Gellie and Stephanie drank tea. Gellie even carried her own tea bags."

Bailey turned to me. "Our tip-off came a few days ago when the crop that's been under surveillance was harvested and sent off to Missouri. That's where I come in, and that's where you came in, too. That freight came directly to this hotel with your name attached to it."

I heard everything he said, but the word "harvested" rang in my ears. Drugs brought to mind powder such as cocaine or heroin. When Bailey had mentioned tea, I'd thought dried material, but we hadn't received anything in a preserved state. Everything had been fresh and newly cut—harvested from the grower and sent to us.

I pictured the flowers in the basement, but knew of none that would be of interest to a drug dealer. The assortment of blossoms was among any florist's inventory. All were famil-iar—except for the shipment from California. It was those shiny green leaves with the bronze tips and the woody stems that had interested Bailey—green leaves for grazing like a cow.

I said, "An unscheduled delivery arrived from California the night of the introductory dinner. In the box was the shiny foliage you spotted in the cooler—the greens you requested to go with the cut flowers you needed for the bogus butterfly display." I looked at Bailey. "Is that what you're talking about?"

He had "staring and not answering my questions" down to a fine art.

"My name was on the packing label because I'm coordinator of the contest. If you'll look at all the boxes that were delivered, I'm sure you'll see my name on each one."

"Who had control over what was sent?"

"Everything we're using is donated. I don't have any say. The suppliers put together what they want, and in exchange, I give them an advertising plug during the actual contest."

"How many suppliers?"

"There are three fresh flowers." I gave him the business names.

"I've checked them," said Bailey.

"The other suppliers are glassware, floral mechanics—wire, ribbon, foam, baskets—that sort of thing."

"What if you wanted something specific, how do you go about getting it?"

"Call them and ask. Each has his own source, but I have no idea who it is. I give my order, and somewhere in the world those flowers are available, if I'm willing to pay the price."

Goose bumps pricked my skin. I was saying word for word what Tyrone had said to us at the introductory dinner.

Robbee had made the connection, too. We stared at each other. "Tyrone?" I said softly. "Is he involved in this?"

"He was at the Fleur-De-Lis Extravaganza," said Robbee, then he shook his head. "But I can't see Tyrone taking the time to talk to Stephanie. She wasn't exactly his type."

"Wouldn't that depend on what he had in mind?" I asked. I looked at Bailey. "What is this khat?" Remembering Gellie's actions and subsequent death, I added, "Is it a hallucinogenic?"

Bailey fought an inner battle, the struggle reflected on his face. He didn't want to give us information, but he needed our cooperation. I knew it was tit-for-tat so I urged him along.

"Robbee, Effie, and I know most of our colleagues personally. We might be able to help you narrow the list of suspects if we knew more about this drug."

Reluctantly Bailey explained, "Khat is a natural stimulant from the *Catha edulis* plant that is found in East Africa and southern Arabia. The fresh leaves contain cathinone, which is chemically similar to d-amphetamine, and cathine, a milder form of cathinone. The khat can also be sold as dried or crushed leaves. It's become increasingly available in the U.S., especially in cities like New York, Los Angeles, Boston, Dallas, and Detroit, where Yemenites have immigrated."

"Are the leaves boiled and the liquid drank?"

"Sometimes the leaves are dried first, then, yes, boiled and seeped into tea. The preference is chewing the tender shoots like tobacco."

"What are the effects after ingesting it?" I asked.

"Alleviation of fatigue. Increased levels of alertness, confidence, contentment with enhanced motor activity. It lifts the spirits, sharpens thinking, dispels hunger, and makes communication easier."

"Sounds like the elixir I used to take," said Effie. "I stopped when I read the label and found it was twenty-five percent alcohol."

Bailey frowned at the interruption. "Now for the downside. It produces grandiose delusions, insomnia, anorexia, breathing difficulties, increased blood pressure and heart rate. When the effects wear off, it generates lapses of depression similar to those of cocaine users.

"Recently, the DEA changed the classification of khat to a schedule I substance, which is the most restrictive category, because of the cathinone, an ingredient present only in the fresh-picked leaves. We don't see khat replacing coke or crack as the next popular street drug. It's too hard to keep in its fresh form unless it's refrigerated, and dealers don't always have that convenience. After forty-eight hours khat loses its potency, unless it's dried and packaged."

"So that foliage in the basement is worth big bucks?" asked Robbee.

Bailey shrugged. "Our street people say the going price is about three to four hundred dollars a kilo, with a bundle of leaves selling for about thirty to fifty dollars."

"That doesn't sound like enough money to make it worth tangling with you guys," said Robbee.

I grimaced. "But you're looking at street value, Robbee. What if the dealer made the use of the drug so desirable to his perspective customer that he or she would be willing to pay any price? You mentioned a loss of appetite, Bailey. How much of a loss?"

Bailey appraised me with something that closely resembled

amazement. "I'm not aware of any studies on the subject, but how did *you* know that's the angle I'm looking at?"

"I don't *know* anything, but I suspect plenty. Because my name was on that delivery of khat, you investigated me. Effie told you I'd lost weight, but I did it the old-fashioned way. I stopped stuffing my face and got up off my wide behind."

Bailey gave me the once over in a slow meandering manner. "I'd say the old-fashioned way did the trick."

I dropped my gaze to the floor so I could concentrate. "What if Stephanie, for her own reasons, decided to lose weight. While she was in Branson, someone approached her with the idea of using this drug. She bought into the plan. What if Gellie was approached, too, but she rejected the idea. She had her stomach stapled instead, but she was regaining the weight she'd lost. This time when she came to Branson, she decided to meet with whoever is involved, bought the drug, and was putting it to use in front of us."

"Good reasoning," said Bailey. "The tea bags found in her room contained dried khat. But she could have brought that stuff with her. I need evidence to connect someone with that shipment in the basement. Do you have something else in mind?"

Quickly I explained about the candy bars in the rest room at Haversham Hall and the plastic bag with the bit of green. "I gave that bag to the officer who questioned me after Gellie's death. If you could do an analysis on that piece of foliage, we'd know if it was khat."

"It's been done. It was."

I huffed. "Well! Why did you ask me if you already knew the answer?"

For the first time since Bailey came out of the closet, his eyes crinkled with humor and his full lips eased into a grin. "I'm still trying to get a handle on how your mind works. Frankly, it's damned scary."

Chapter Nineteen

"Damned scary" or not, Bailey spent more than an hour exploring every crease and crevice of my memory, probing for facts. It was his suggestion that we adjourn to my room for an in-depth discussion.

Effie looked exhausted, but she wouldn't give in to my suggestion that I take her back to her room. She compromised by lying on my bed, propped up with two fluffy pillows. I sat near her. Bailey and Robbee occupied the chairs by the window. We speculated on the association's board of directors and the contestants.

"I think you ought to look into Darren's background," said Robbee for the umpteenth time. "He makes all those trips abroad. He says he's doing design classes, but how do we know he hasn't been cultivating khat clients on the side?"

If Darren could dupe the entire florist industry into believing he was the "great designer," wasn't it possible that he could bamboozle us about the khat? He'd been at the Fleur-De-Lis Extravaganza. He had contacts with people around the world who specialized in growing plants. Perhaps he'd brought the khat to the U.S., set up the farm in California to raise the crop, and then used his fame to make contacts for selling the drug.

"Who owns that farm in California?" I asked Bailey.

"If there's a connection with anyone here, we haven't discovered it. We're in the process of tracing phone numbers, airfare from Missouri to California, but all that takes time. This convention will be over soon, and everyone will go his or her separate way."

"We could wait and see who snatches the khat," said Robbee.

Bailey shrugged. "I doubt the person will make a claim. It'll be chalked up as a loss, and perhaps even the end of the business, unless there are other contacts we haven't discovered."

I sighed. "Stephanie's death was ruled a heart attack, and I would guess since she was overweight that's as far as the coroner took his investigation. Gellie wasn't exactly murdered, but she's dead because she used khat." I looked at Bailey. "Will you tell me the circumstances surrounding the McDuffys' murders?"

"Their bodies were found at the bottom of a ravine. No car was at the scene. Neither of the McDuffys was in condition to walk up the winding, abandoned road, so we have to assume a third person was involved. We found a camera near the couple. The developed photos showed Vincent and Mabel posed with their back to the gorge. The last frame showed the same shot, but without the McDuffys. Putting everything together, we think they were pushed over the edge."

Effie clucked her tongue. I glanced at her and saw her eyes were closed, but she whispered, "Such a sad ending when their lives were already filled with sorrow."

Bailey continued, "Reggie helped recover the bodies after the grisly find was reported to the local authorities. I'd already alerted the Branson chief of police that I was in town and would appreciate his cooperation if anything unusual took place."

"A double homicide would surely qualify as unusual," said Robbee. "But how come none of us heard about it?"

"This was a closed federal investigation. A drug bust. Reggie and I were sent to Branson to see who was on the receiving end of the khat. When the call came in about the McDuffys' murders and we learned that they were from Spencer County, I decided to keep their deaths a secret for as long as possible. At that time, it seemed like the right decision." He shot a glance my way. "My best lead was from Spencer County, too."

That would be me. While I'd gone about my conference duties, I'd been watched by the DEA. No wonder Sid had said I was out of my league.

Bailey was saying, "—we decided that if the killer was under the mistaken impression that the McDuffys' bodies hadn't been found, we'd have a better chance of capturing him. Sheriff Hancock was instructed to cooperate with us."

I was more disgusted than angry. "You got my life history, right? My renovating a historical home. My preference to golden oldie music. My deceased husband, who just happened to be a deputy. Did you think I'd turned to a life of crime since his death?"

"I check out all leads," he said firmly.

"Why were you at the funeral home?" I asked.

"I needed a location where Reggie and I could meet and plan our strategy. I didn't want him here at the hotel. He needed freedom to move about, and I couldn't be seen around the police station. When the bodies were discovered and taken to the funeral home for the coroner's examination, I designated the Eternal Rest Chapel as home base."

I said, "I'm not going to try to dispute your evidence, but something just isn't ringing true here. I never met Vincent and Mabel, but from the tone of the notes they wrote to me, and from my impression of them, I figured they had plenty of spirit. I can't see them going gullibly along with their daughter's killer only to end up at the base of a cliff."

"I think you're on the right track, dear," said Effie, sitting up straight. "The name Vincent comes from the Latin origin meaning 'conquering.' I'd say the man had a plan."

A plan?

Lavelle had described the McDuffys as being good neighbors but overly cautious. Vincent had wanted to shut off the electricity to his house and sell his flock of chickens. I'd wondered if he suspected that they might not be coming home. With Stephanie's death, all Vincent and Mabel had was each other. Lavelle was worried about Vincent when Mabel passed on. I frowned. I wished that I'd had the chance to meet them, then I could have formed my own opinion of the kind of people they had been. However, there was another possibility if Bailey would agree.

I asked, "Do you have those photos of the McDuffys that were taken at the top of the ravine?" When he nodded, I leaned eagerly toward him. "Please let me look at them."

Hearing the intensity in my voice, he said, "First rule of being a skilled detective, Bretta, is to keep your distance. Don't become emotionally involved." He pulled an envelope from his breast pocket and held it out to me. "After twenty-eight years, I'm breaking that rule."

Was he talking about the case or becoming emotionally involved with me? I had my answer when I took the envelope. My fingers brushed his and the brief contact made my skin tingle. Did he feel it? Did he have any personal feelings for me? I looked into his coppery eyes and saw them sparkle.

In a droll tone, Robbee asked, "Should Effie and I step into the hall for twenty minutes?"

My cheeks burned with embarrassment. "Shut up, Robbee," I said as I went to my purse and removed the five-by-seven envelope the McDuffys had given me. When I took it to Bailey, I couldn't meet his gaze, and I didn't have the stamina to chance touching his hand again.

I laid the envelope on the table between him and Robbee. "That's from the McDuffys," I said. "The contents are exactly as I found them." I sat down on the bed.

Bailey left the envelope lying on the table, but when Robbee reached for it, the look he received was pure "special agent supremacy" and as effective as a slap on the wrist. "Go ahead, Bretta," said Bailey, "look at the pictures. The one is of the McDuffys. The other is a faxed printout of a photo Sheriff Hancock found when he went to their house. From the date on the back it was taken a few weeks before Stephanie passed away."

As I drew them out, Effie scrambled so she could see. Robbee crossed the carpet and plopped down next to me. Both of them peered over my shoulder. I unfolded the faxed picture first. It was black and white, blurred, and smudged around the edges. Stephanie was dressed in a skirt. Her blouse had a Victorian collar that framed her pretty face. The tail of her blouse was smoothly tucked into the narrow waistband of her dark skirt.

"Good Lord," said Robbee. "She's gorgeous. Check out those fabulous cheekbones." He leaned closer, studying the paper intently. "I can't believe it's the same woman."

"Yeah," I said. "Stephanie looks great, but notice the way she's hanging on to that chair? The woman is so weak she can hardly stand up." I would have put the picture back in the envelope, but Robbee took it, staring as if mesmerized.

The other photo was clear and sharp. The Ozark Mountains in the background were lovely, but the subjects at the forefront might've been comical if they weren't so heartbreaking. Mabel's emaciated body was wrapped in the curve of her husband's arm. Vincent McDuffy was enormous. Suspenders held up a pair of pants that looked as if they'd been painted on his massive frame. His eyes were sunk into pockets of fatty tissue. The unrelenting stare he directed into the camera's lens made me squirm.

The death of a loved one is an emotional trauma that tears at the heart and ravages the brain. To find some measure of peace, people often turn to their faith in God. I figured the McDuffys had found solace in another area. They'd put aside their grief and plotted revenge against the person who'd caused their daughter's death. They'd come to Branson for a deadly confrontation. Stephanie was gone. Mabel was dying. Vincent would be alone.

I swallowed. They had nothing to lose.

"Bailey, you said the DEA has changed the category of khat to a schedule I drug, but if the McDuffys weren't dead, what kind of sentence are we talking about?"

"Depends on the judge and the deftness of the lawyer the dealer hires. If this dealer hasn't any priors, his lawyer might use the fact that he or she was trying to help obese women lose weight. That's the defense I'd use, and the end result might be a slap on the wrist, pay out a fine, and go on probation."

"It would be pretty tough to pin Stephanie's death or Gellie's, for that matter, on the drug. Stephanie's weight could have brought on a heart condition that none of them were aware of until it was too late."

Bailey asked, "Where are you going with this?"

"As far as I'm concerned, both women were murdered. The dealer preyed on their vulnerability. When a person is as obese as each of these women were, they would've seized on drastic measures, not giving a thought to the consequences. I can understand their reasoning, but there's always a chance that a judge or a jury might not see it as such."

Bailey plucked his lower lip thoughtfully. The simple gesture was sensuous and called to mind the brief touch of his lips against mine. What would it be like to be held by this man and thoroughly kissed?

"Go on," murmured Bailey.

My eyes widened in confusion until I recalled my original train of thought. Still I hesitated, but now for another reason. His steady gaze was on me. I didn't understand why I was drawn to this man, when I knew so little about him. But the attraction was there, and had been since I'd seen him in the lobby. I wanted the chance to get to know him better, to sort out what was the true Bailey Monroe, and what had been his cover for this operation. What I said next would test which way our relationship might go. If he scoffed at me, I'd have my answer. But if he listened—

I took the plunge. "I'm talking about a suicide pact between Mabel and Vincent." Bailey's eyebrows drew down, but I hurried on, "No, don't say anything. Hear me out. The McDuffys knew that their daughter met someone in Branson. In their letter to me they said that their daughter had been led astray. They came to town to find that someone, but I don't think they were interested in having him arrested for dealing the drug. I think Vincent had something else in mind."

Robbee shook his head. "That's pretty far-fetched, Bretta."

"But it fits," said Effie. "Vincent McDuffy—conquering his foe."

"It isn't far-fetched at all," I said to Robbee. "Consider the facts. Bailey just said that the dealer might get a slap on the wrist, but murder—a double homicide—would result in more than a reprimand." I touched the photo. "Mabel doesn't look as if she's long for this world. Vincent is a time bomb. His heart won't take much more abuse. They loved each other. Life for the one that was left would have been unbearable. They lost their daughter to this drug, which would be hard to prove. But if they could entice the dealer into killing them, what better way to bring about retribution for Stephanie's death?"

"I don't know," muttered Robbee. "Seems to me you're hinging everything on their love for each other." He snorted. "That emotion gets too much press, as far as I'm concerned."

"Only because you've never experienced it, dear." Effie's eyes were shiny with tears. "When two people find each other, whether their relationship remains a friendship or leads to something more serious, they should cherish that alliance."

I sat silent, waiting for Bailey to speak. He took his time, staring off into space. I assumed he was mulling over the evidence. I forced myself not to prod him with any more of my conjectures. When I was ready to give up, Bailey reached down to his penny loafers and reverently touched each dime.

"My wife and I celebrated twenty years together," he said quietly. "On our last anniversary she gave me these two dimes taped in a card. A week later she was killed in a car crash. One dime is from the year I was born. The other is hers." He cleared his throat roughly. "She was a romantic, sentimental woman. I loved her beyond reason. When she died, I wanted to die, too."

Bailey looked up. His gaze rested on my lips. "We'll never know what was in Vincent's mind, Bretta," said Bailey softly. "You and I have both experienced what it's like to lose someone we love. Based on that, I'd say your assumption is possible. However one fact hasn't changed."

His voice deepened with authority. "Someone has been distributing an illegal drug. That's the person I'm after. And if I net a killer in the bargain, so much the better. Let's get the bastard."

Chapter Twenty

Saturday morning dawned with clear skies. The sun rose above the horizon, shedding its brilliance over the land, chasing away shadows that blurred the imagination. I hoped the light of day would reveal answers, just as it was exposing the familiar landmarks that were outside my window.

The miniature golf course appeared deserted. It was 6:00 A.M., but I'd noticed during my stay at the hotel that workmen usually congregated outside the gates by this time. I leaned closer and saw a banner stretched between two posts. GRAND OPENING—SUNDAY, MAY 1. The golf course would open a week from tomorrow. By that time, I'd be back home, in my same old rut, and I hoped a murderer would be in jail.

My eyes burned from lack of sleep. I reached up to rub them, but remembered in time that I'd already applied my makeup. Wearily, I closed my eyes and leaned against the chair Bailey had occupied last night. I was dressed for the contest—mauve suit, a floral-print blouse, hose, and flats. Heels were out. I'd be on my feet all day.

I opened my eyes and touched the chair cushion where Bailey had rested his head. If Robbee and Effie hadn't been in the room last night, I wondered what might have happened between Bailey and me. Maybe nothing, but then again . . . His gaze on my lips had spoken of a promise. Or was I merely hoping? I couldn't toss my memories of Carl aside, but they were only—memories. Bailey represented a new course in my life, if I had the nerve to pursue it.

I stood up straight and squared my shoulders. My thoughts were premature. First I had to get through my responsibilities as coordinator for the floral contest. I reached under the mattress for my notebook and CD and stuffed them into my bulging handbag.

Not long ago, this contest had been vastly important. Now it was merely the backdrop for a sinister plot that had resulted in four deaths. Were there other victims? How many people had been persuaded to use this khat? How far-reaching was the drug? Could it be traced back to a florist, to one of my colleagues?

Effie was to meet me downstairs for some last-minute details before the contest began at ten o'clock. Allison, Bernice, and Tyrone would be there, too. So would Chloe, Miriam, Zach, and Robbee. Before he left my room last night, I'd given Robbee the go-ahead to participate as a contestant. I'd expected jubilation, but his response had been low-key. A different priority rested on his shoulders.

Bailey had told us to continue with the conference as if nothing was amiss. We weren't to ask questions—this was stressed with another "special agent" look. Above all, we were to act normal toward everyone involved in the conference.

I passed on the stairs and rode down to the lobby in the elevator. Catching my reflection in the glass panel, I smoothed my skirt over my hips and thought about the khat. On the surface it seemed admirable that someone had tried to help obese women lose weight.

Admirable? I'd paid that compliment recently. I frowned but couldn't make the association. My thoughts skipped on.

Wouldn't it be wonderful if the plant worked healthfully? There had been times in my life when I might have bought into the drug. By chewing some leaves the appetite would disappear, and the excess weight would melt off. It sounded too good to be true—and it was.

The elevator bell dinged, and I stepped into the lobby. The main conference doors had been tied shut with a bright red bow. I took the service hall and stepped into the meeting room, expecting to see Effie fluttering about checking bouquets for water.

Robbee, dressed in a suit and tie, was tidying up with a whisk broom and dustpan. The casket was gone, and in its place was the trophy among the display of sympathy arrangements.

"What do you think?" he asked, catching sight of me.

"It doesn't have the 'grabber' effect I'd hoped for with the casket, but in light of all that's happened, it'll be fine."

"Alvin and three of the hotel employees helped me bring the flowers up from the basement." He gave me a significant look. "We brought *everything* up."

I stepped through the connecting doorway. Robbee had switched on the spotlights that were aimed at the tables spaced across the front of the room. My gaze zeroed in on the glossy foliage sitting among the colorful blossoms. The obnoxious leaves appeared to shimmer in the bright lights. Now that I knew what it was, I wanted a closer look but resisted the urge.

"Have you seen Effie?" I asked.

"Not since I escorted her to her room last night."

I shifted my handbag so I could see my watch. "She's late. I wonder if she overslept? She was exhausted when she left my room." Worry set in. "You hold down the fort. I'm going upstairs to check on her."

I walked out of the contest room, down the service hall, and to the stairwell that was closer. I had my hand on the doorknob when I felt an uncomfortable tingling of the skin on my neck. When I glanced around Bernice stared at me with loathing.

I spun on my heel and went to the elevators. The hotel was coming alive, and I had to wait for my ride up to the second floor. It was a tedious delay—one I could have forgone if I'd had the nerve to use the stairs.

When I was in the glass box, I looked down on the lobby for Bernice. She was where I'd last seen her, watching my every move.

Was she furious because I'd upstaged Tyrone last night? She'd been the one to call my attention to the California delivery. Was her constant haggling about money a blind to her distributing the khat?

Stepping out of the elevator, I repeated a comment Bailey had made to me. "It always comes back to money."

Selling drugs usually equates to a financial gain. But was money the only issue? A criminal's persona was built upon layers and layers of personality defects and past occurrences. The first step in bringing him or her to justice was to peel away the veneer that covered the outer facade, much as Stephanie had done in her artwork.

From the moment I'd seen the picture on the armoire in the McDuffys' room, I'd felt that they'd brought it with them for a reason. In my mind, I went back over each caricature, aligning it with the facts Bailey had revealed. The green leaves that Gellie had been holding could represent the khat. Was there another clue?

I had recognized each person, either by a physical characteristic or a personality flaw. Stephanie had captured their essence in her portrayals. I frowned. Except for one. Why had Stephanie used an onion skin in her depiction of Alvin?

The pulse at the base of my throat beat an erratic tempo. Alvin? I hadn't considered him a suspect, and yet, hadn't my subconscious been alerted? An onion consisted of concentric layers, the skin a fragile veneer.

As I rapped on Effie's door, I let my thoughts flow. Bailey had said that the khat was from Africa. Was Alvin using drug money to help that orphanage in Somalia? I nodded slowly as pieces drifted into place. Alvin was the one whose actions I'd said were admirable.

It's always the least suspected. African tea. Somalia orphanage. Obese women. Starving children. Starve—die. That's what my weary mind had spun on last night in bed when I couldn't sleep.

I knocked harder on the door. "Effie? Are you awake?" I put my ear to the panel but heard no movement on the other side.

"What's wrong, Bretta?"

I swung around and saw Alvin hurrying along the balcony toward me. I stiffened, then forced myself to relax and smile naturally. I had to hide my suspicions, and think of Alvin as the nice man who'd assisted me with the conference. Not the one who might be responsible for four deaths.

"It's Effie," I explained. "She was supposed to meet me downstairs but didn't. I'm worried about her."

"I have a master key, but I'm not supposed to use it except in case of emergency."

"This is an emergency."

"All right," said Alvin, pulling the plastic card from his pocket. "If we surprise her getting out of the shower, you take the responsibility. Okay?"

I agreed, and Alvin swung the door open. I hurried inside. The bed was made, the draperies pushed back to let the sun in. The bathroom was empty. Papers littered a small table by the windows. I stepped closer and examined them. Nothing but her notes for the conference.

"We might as well go downstairs," I said. "Perhaps she's in the café. I should have checked before coming up here."

"Are you all right?"

My gaze slid across his face. "It's this contest. I need Effie's help and it isn't like her not to be around." I forced my stiff lips into a semblance of a smile. "Robbee told me that you and some of the staff helped him bring everything up from the basement. I'd better go do my part. Effie will show up before long."

I took two steps to the door, but stopped when Alvin said, "I understand you've lost a considerable amount of weight. Are you having trouble keeping it off?"

Brushing the hair off my damp forehead, I glanced around. Alvin stood with his back to me, staring out the window. I wasn't sure where this conversation was headed, but I played along. "I have my days. Remember how I devoured the snacks you had sent to us when we were cutting flower stems the other night?"

"Not flowers, Bretta." Alvin turned. "Those bronze leaves are an effective tool for weight loss and controlling your appetite. Yemenites and East African natives chew the tender shoots. I usually dry the leaves before packaging the mixture into bags for my clients. It makes shipment easier, and they can get a cup of hot water most anywhere when hunger attacks."

I worked my way closer to the door. "And it grows in California?"

"It isn't indigenous to the area, but southern California's weather parallels East Africa or southern Arabia, so the plants have done fairly well. Ben, my grower, was with me in the Peace Corps. He and his team tried to teach the natives how to raise nourishing crops, but conditions were deplorable. He became as sickened as I did at the sight of fellow human beings barely existing, and the children who don't stand a chance."

Alvin stared at the carpet. "I didn't know Ben had smuggled plants into the U.S. until I received the box of the foliage. I recognized the leaves, having seen them used as a recreational and religious drug. Ben proposed the plan for the orphanage in Somalia. As a blind for receiving the shipment of foliage, I suggested fresh flowers for the hotel. When your florist convention picked this location, I decided it would be a convenient time to receive an even larger shipment. With all your flowers arriving, who'd notice an extra box of greens?"

I licked my dry lips. "Why are you telling me this?"

"Because I understand from Helen that you've been asking lots of questions. I have the answers. The McDuffys checked into the hotel, then spent hours in the lobby watching me. That first day I went up to them and asked if I could help them. That's when I learned they believed I was responsible for Stephanie's death. I walked away, but they continued to watch me whenever I was nearby.

"After four days, I'd had enough. I invited them to go on a sightseeing trip. I was sorry for their loss, but there was more at stake than their grief. I met them at the side entrance of the hotel, and we took my car up to a particularly lovely area. It helped that I'd taken Stephanie there because she'd described the view to her parents, and they were willing to go with me."

Alvin dashed a hand across his face. "I didn't take them up there to kill them, Bretta, but when it came down to being exposed by the McDuffys or getting rid of them—I chose the latter."

From the way Alvin was talking, I didn't think he knew about the DEA investigation. Bailey was my ace in the hole. If Alvin didn't know about Bailey, then perhaps he wouldn't become desperate to murder again.

I took another step toward the door. "I'm leaving."

"I can't keep you here."

Why would Alvin feed me these details only to let me walk away? Whatever his reasoning, I had to find Bailey. I hurried to the door and had even turned the knob when Alvin spoke again.

"Just one more thing. Effie is tied up—literally. I wouldn't count on her assistance for the contest."

Chapter Twenty-one

Alvin's humdrum delivery concerning Effie took a moment to register. When it did, my chin shot up, my eyes widened with disbelief. "My God, you *are* a monster. Where is she? What have you done to her?"

"I know it'll be difficult carrying on with your conference duties, but if you want Effie to live, you don't have a choice."

"There are always choices."

"Not this time if you value the life of your friend."

"Friend?" I nearly screeched the word. "What would you know about being a friend?" I forced myself to calm down and speak quietly. "Staging the benefits each year is commendable. Your intentions were selfless, but you've tainted all the good you could've done. Let Effie go. She's just a sweet, little old lady."

"The McDuffys were good people, too," said Alvin. "But Mabel was dying. Vincent wouldn't have lasted much longer. I think they expected me to do something. That look in Vincent's eyes, just before he went over the edge of the bluff, has haunted me. It was as if he was satisfied by the turn of events."

"He pressed you into killing them because he was afraid nothing could be proved about Stephanie's death."

"You're sharp, Bretta. Sharp as a razor blade."

Startled, I jerked upright.

Alvin nodded. "Yeah, those little gifts came from me. I didn't want to maim you, but only slow you down. You've complicated everything, but I've decided that's par for the course when you're around. You get involved. You're too soft-hearted for your own good, but that's my mulligan—a free shot at this game. Effie will be found when this conference is over, if you don't go against my instructions."

"What instructions?"

"Continue with the conference. Keep your mouth shut or you'll bogie yourself into a sand trap." Alvin moved past me, opened the door, then calmly walked away.

I hurried after him and watched him saunter to the elevators. Before he entered the box, he turned, daring me to stop him. I met his gaze but did nothing until he was on the elevator.

I went to the balcony and leaned over the railing, searching for Bailey. I spotted him outside the souvenir shop. He appeared to be waiting for a companion, glancing impatiently at his wristwatch.

Alvin got off the elevator and crossed the lobby. He waved jauntily to the woman at the front desk before going out the front doors of the hotel.

What was I to do? If I told Bailey about Alvin, would he spring into action? Would he see apprehending Alvin as more important than Effie's safety? Last night he'd said, "Let's get the bastard." I'd taken the statement as camaraderie—banding together to right a wrong. But what if Bailey had meant it as a gung-ho macho remark—not letting anything or anyone get in his path? I was attracted to Bailey, but I didn't know him. If it were Carl in Bailey's place, he'd make sure Effie was unharmed before he went after Alvin.

But there was no Carl, and time was running out. I could sit tight, say nothing, and hope that Alvin had told the truth and Effie would be free when the conference ended. But that would be tomorrow evening. If he were lying, then hours would have passed with Effie enduring God knows what.

With my head bowed in thought I rode the elevator to the lobby. I'd hardly stepped out of the car when Bailey was at my side.

"I've been waiting for you," he said, taking my elbow and leading me to a quiet corner. "Robbee said you went up to check on Effie. Is she all right?"

"I hope so."

Bailey squeezed my arm. "What's wrong? Wasn't she in her room?"

"No," I said, turning away from the concern in his eyes. Was I misjudging Bailey? I hardened my "soft" heart. Alvin had said to keep my mouth shut.

"She's probably wandering around the hotel looking for you." He lowered his head so he could stare into my face. "Something's wrong. Is it Effie? Do you want me to look for her?"

"Yes. Would you see if she's here in the hotel?" I gestured to the crowd of florists that were already gathering in the lobby for the contest. "I need some air. While I'm outside, I'll check to see if her little car is in the parking lot."

"Okay," said Bailey, flashing me a smile. "Got a case of nerves about the contest?" He winked. "You'll do fine. I'll meet you in this general area in about twenty minutes." He squeezed my arm again before moving off.

After he'd disappeared into the crowd, I went outside. The smell of spring quickened the blood in my veins. I drew a deep breath. The sun had gilded the landscape. Clouds skimmed across a sky that was as blue as a morning-glory blossom.

My gaze circled the parking lot for Effie's car. It was there. I eyed the hotel. Alvin had said she was "tied up—literally." With his master key, he had access to any empty room in the nine-story building. I stared up the hill to Haversham Hall and the conservatory—more rooms, more space. I would need an army to make a thorough search. Behind me the miniature golf course was ready and waiting for its grand opening next week.

Golf course? Alvin had peppered his appraisal of my character with golfing terms. "Par for the course." "Mulligan." "Bogie." "Sand trap." Or was he setting a trap for me? I gritted my teeth. That's a stupid question.

I crossed the parking lot to the admittance gate. It was unlatched. "How convenient?" I murmured, stepping through the opening. My uneasiness at entering the course was outranked by the need to make sure Effie was safe. I hadn't intentionally drawn her into danger, but my actions had played a major role. She'd attached herself to my heart, and I wasn't about to let anything happen to her.

There were eighteen different attractions on this course. I knew the layout from having looked down on it from my hotel room. The only place where Effie could be hidden from view was in the cave, which the hotel brochure boasted as being a "real tourist treat."

I worked my way toward the fourteenth hole, taking the twisting path of green carpet-covered walks. Even in my harried state, I could see there was plenty of potential for this theme park becoming a popular stopping place. No expense had been spared when it came to the plantings. Beds of tulips, narcissus, daffodils, and crocus were tucked into a thick layer of mulch. Forsythia, pussywillow bushes, and Bradford pear trees were coming into bloom. Around each corner, statues of noted Missourians—Walt Disney, Laura Ingalls Wilder, Mark Twain, George Washington Carver, Harry S. Truman, and Scott Joplin—were incorporated into the challenge of sinking a putt.

I hastened under the replica of the St. Louis arch that loomed twenty-five feet in the air—far short of the six hundred and thirty foot rise of the original. Laminated signs guided me down a ramp and gave a historical background of the two-chamber cave. I skipped over the chronicle, concentrating on the map.

Directly in front of me was the chamber where the golfer would find his fourteenth putt. The main attraction involved taking a winding corridor that looped like an intestine into the bowels of the earth and ended in a colon-shaped cavern. According to the hype, by taking this "special tour" my "senses would be titillated by the atmospheric conditions." I wasn't sure I could handle "titillated" on top of just plain scared.

As I entered the dimly lit hole, the sudden change in temperature made me shiver. I walked the golf green to the fourteenth hole. Colored lights guided me around unusual rock formations. Stalactites hung from the ceiling, while stalagmites rose from the floor like evil spears waiting to impale an imprudent visitor.

It took only a few seconds to see that Effie wasn't in this first chamber. I followed directional arrows to the entrance for the special tour and stepped to the opening.

"Effie?" I called into the dark cavern. An eerie silence greeted me. I strained my ears when I picked up a faraway cry. "Effie?"

"Leave!" she shouted.

Alvin's mocking voice filled the air. "But you won't, will

you? You're a predictable woman, Bretta Solomon. I knew you'd figure it out, and here you are."

It sounded as if Alvin was speaking over an intercom, so he could be anywhere. "What do you want me to do?" I asked.

"Take the tour, of course."

"And if I don't?"

I heard what sounded like a smack. Effie cried out in pain.

"No! No!" I shouted. "I'm coming in."

"I thought you would," was Alvin's soft reply.

With heart pounding, I took a step into the blackness. A network of twinkle lights came on, crisscrossing the ceiling like a million tiny stars. Reassured by the festive, almost frivolous sight, I slung the strap of my handbag over my shoulder and navigated the first stretch of corridor that was eight feet wide.

I rounded a bend and heard a far-off rumble. I choked back a cry of surprise when the twinkle lights dimmed, then went out. Lightning flashed across the ceiling in a jagged streak followed by another menacing rumble. Pictures projected on the walls drew me into a violent thunderstorm. Bolts of electricity sliced the darkness, splitting it and exposing clouds that were green and ominous. Hailstones the size of grapefruit pounded craters into the earth, stripped trees of their leaves. The scene abruptly switched to an expensive brick house. Pellets of ice smashed through the bay windows, shattering the glass, sending lethal shards in all directions.

When the storm died away, and the lights had come back on, I leaned against the wall, willing my heart to behave.

Alvin's voice surrounded me. "Wasn't that a treat, Bretta? I've never understood why tourists pay money to have the bejabbers scared out of them. Keep walking."

I crept down the passage like a soldier on patrol, looking first to my left and then to my right. Without warning the lights went out, but under my feet a five-by-ten-foot square of glass was lit. Water rumbled by with simulated people caught in the flood.

I stared in horror as their bodies helplessly fought the crashing waves. Piercing screams for help echoed off the stone walls. The faces turned up to me were so lifelike, so in need of rescuing, I nearly burst into tears at their plight and mine. Then without warning the floor reverted to darkness, but the twinkle lights didn't come on.

I waited, praying that the blackness would be broken by their glow, but no comforting light appeared. My breath came in painful gasps. My chest ached with tension. These were minor concerns, as Alvin once again spoke.

"Effie looks lovely today, Bretta. She's dressed in purple. Wonder if she'd bleed purple, too."

A sob worked its way up my throat, and I cried, "Please, don't hurt her."

"That's up to you, isn't it?"

I clenched my jaws. He's baiting you, I thought wildly. Keep control. Keep moving forward. I pictured the map in my mind. How many twists of the corridor before I reached the final cavern? Five? Six? How many had I already passed? Three? Four?

A gentle breeze against my face alerted me that another production was in the making. I moved to my left, hugging the damp stone wall, sidling slowly. The breeze turned to a swift flow of air. A lit sign flashed the words—TORNADO ALLEY. Jets of air swooshed past me. A roar like a freight train filled the corridor. The sound escalated until my head throbbed with the pulsation.

I cowered, panting in terror. Images flashed on the rock walls—trees uprooted, houses torn apart, and shingles flew through the air like guided missiles. Sheets of tin, ripped off an old barn, carried the threat of decapitation. It was as if I were in the tornado funnel. The sights, the sounds, and even the smell that permeated the air reeked of death and destruction.

Abruptly the storm ended. I walked another twenty feet, and a ball of hot light shone down on me. I wiggled uncomfortably. The heat was intense. I squinted against the glare.

Alvin's whisper chilled me. "It feels like hell, doesn't it, Bretta? Hell hath no fury like a woman on my trail. You're getting closer."

I stepped up my pace, but I wondered what was next in this cave of meteorological horrors. I'd been subjected to everything Missouri had to offer in the weather department. I took another twist in the corridor and came to a dead stop at the entrance to the second chamber.

Photographs of huge, fluffy white clouds floated against a cerulean ceiling. From a recording, birds chirruped a cheerful serenade. A mist system spewed droplets that created a rainbow of such vivid hues it hurt my eyes. But the sight that made me pause was Effie.

She was seated in a captain's chair, dressed in a lovely orchid suit with a frilly blouse. A brooch adorned her lapel and earrings sparkled on her tiny ears. Both of her legs and her right arm were tied to the chair. Her left hand was free, but her fingertips had been wrapped with duct tape, making any attempt at freeing herself clumsy if not impossible. Her eyes were closed, her head rested against the back of the chair, an open book lay across her lap.

Before I went to her, I searched the cavern for Alvin. Where was he? There had to be a control booth where all the technical apparatus was kept. I looked back at Effie. She'd spotted me and was trying to smile.

Cautiously, I crossed to her side. "Where is he?" I whispered as I fumbled with the knots that bound her legs.

She licked her lips. "I don't know."

"I'm sorry this happened. Why did you leave the hotel?"

"Alvin said you were in trouble. I didn't hesitate coming with him. I'm a gullible old lady, and I should have a keeper."

I finished the last knot as a lone tear rolled down her wrinkled cheek.

"He was kind. He even apologized for tying me, but he didn't make allowances for an old woman's weak bladder. I tried to hold it, but I couldn't." Another tear followed the last. "I've ruined my clothes. What will I wear for the contest?"

"We can't worry about that now," I said, helping her out of the chair. Once Effie was on her feet, she swayed weakly, and I put my arm around her narrow waist. "We have to get out of here."

We'd taken only a few steps when the recorded bird chirps ceased. The mist spray dwindled to a spurt. The rainbow dissolved into nothingness.

"Going so soon?" asked Alvin.

This time he wasn't speaking over an intercom. I jerked around. My gaze darted to an outcropping of rocks some twenty feet away. As I watched, he moved steadily in our direction.

"Bretta," he said, shaking his head, "your compassion for others is to be commended—but not this time."

I urged Effie toward the corridor, but spoke to Alvin. "Let her go. She doesn't understand what this is about."

"But, dear, I do," said Effie, waving the book that had been in her lap.

I caught a glimpse of the title: *Historical Names and Their Reference* and sensed what was coming. I attempted to shush her, but she wouldn't keep still.

"The name 'Alvin' has an old German origin meaning a friend to all. He's the killer, dear, and he's done just as you predicted. He's slithered out of hiding."

Chapter Twenty-two

Alvin's eyes narrowed. "Slithered? That's rather crude, don't you think?"

"Let Effie go."

"I can't," he said, pulling something from his pocket.

I watched his hand. Saw his thumb make a sliding motion. When he held up a box cutter, I didn't make a sound, but my body tightened with tension. The words "slice and dice" ripped through my brain. "Don't do this," I said, eyeing the blade.

Effie swayed. "I'm dizzy."

"Hold on," I said, tightening my grip on her waist. I made another appeal to Alvin. "Please, let her go so she can see a doctor."

"No. Put her back in that chair."

"She needs medical attention."

Effie patted my hand. "I won't leave you, dear. I'll be all right." She glared at Alvin. "But I will accept your offer to sit again."

"Then get over there," he said.

Leaning heavily on my arm, Effie shuffled a couple of steps. Suddenly she gasped. The book slipped from her hands and hit the cave floor with a thud. "Oh," she moaned, pressing a hand to her breast. "Oh!"

I tried to catch her, but my handbag got in the way. I tossed it aside, but she slid out of my grasp. Tears filled my eyes as I knelt at her side. "Effie? Effie?" I called frantically.

I put my head to her chest and heard the steady beat of her heart. I focused on her face and saw the color rise in her wrinkled cheeks. I dashed a hand at my tears and nearly missed seeing her eye flutter in a sly wink.

Good Lord above. She was up to something.

"No!" I screeched. "Hell, no," I added for emphasis.

Alvin mistook my ranting as grief. "Is she dead?"

I used my body to shield Effie from his gaze. "Her life is hanging by a thread. Let me take her out of here."

"You've overworked that plea. Let her die peacefully." He motioned to me. "Get over here. You have a different fate."

This time I moved quickly. I wanted his attention off Effie. I didn't know what she had in mind, but if Alvin saw she was faking it—I gulped and circled the area coming up on his left.

"Stop right there," he said, aiming the box cutter at my throat. "I want you to soak your feet in that pool of water."

I followed the direction he indicated. The runoff from the mist system had created more than a rainbow. A good-sized puddle had formed in a hollow on the stone floor. "Why?" I asked.

"Just do it. Get your feet wet, then move along to the corridor."

I stared down at the water, trying to buy time. "Should I take my shoes off?"

"Are the soles rubber?"

My eyes widened. I peered over my shoulder, seeing the twinkle lights from a different perspective. The thousands of tiny bulbs had seemed so reassuring, so festive. Now they shone with a perilous glow. So many interconnecting wires, so much electricity.

I shuffled a step away, but Alvin shoved me. I stumbled and fell to my knees. The stone floor tore my hose and scraped away tender flesh. Water splashed my face and soaked my skirt.

Alvin said, "That ought to do it. Get up." For an added incentive, he put the razor to my cheek. "Now."

I struggled painfully to my feet, bedraggled and furious. Without thinking, I lashed out, wanting to wipe the sneer from his face. He put his hand up, and the blade sliced through my sleeve and into my arm. It happened so smoothly and so quickly, I didn't realize I'd been wounded until I felt the blood run down my wrist. I stared at the scarlet flow in disbelief.

"I mean business," said Alvin.

I looked at him, then past him, and fought to control my expression. Effie was on her knees, her butt in the air. She clawed at my purse, trying to draw it closer. She was so focused that she wasn't watching Alvin.

What if he heard her?

What if he turned around?

I seized a topic out of thin air and babbled like a brook after a downpour. "You're not going to get away with killing me. I have that floral contest to conduct. If I'm not back at the hotel when the conference doors open, this entire complex will be crawling with angry florists searching for me. And this group won't give up."

Effie had my purse in hand and was slowly rising to her feet. I tried for a cool, confident laugh, but it came out a high-pitched cackle. "Florists are resourceful, too," I said, plowing on. "Someone will figure out where I am."

Step by step, Effie crept toward us.

"They'll storm this golf course so fast you won't know what—"

Alvin raised the blade. "Shut up."

Effie was six feet from her target. Her mouth was pursed in a grim line. Slowly, she raised her arm.

Alvin started to turn his head, but I flipped my hand under his nose to gain his attention. "Yeah, that's what a florist is—resourceful. When a customer asks for something clever and ingenuous, we deliver. We aim to please. We don't duck our responsibilities. We clobber the competition."

"God, but you are annoying," said Alvin, slapping at my hand. "You're wasting time."

"TIME!" I screamed.

Effie's eyes shone with determination as she swung my loaded handbag at Alvin. Because she was short and the bag was heavy, her aim was a tad off. The blow missed his head, but slammed into his shoulder, knocking him off balance. The box cutter flew out of his hand and clattered somewhere to my right.

Not to be outdone by this feisty woman, I added my fury to the fracas.

I hit low . . . I hit hard . . . I hit dirty. Alvin folded like the leaves of a prayer plant at dusk.

From what I understood of the male anatomy, my punch to the soft tissue of his groin should've put him out of commission. But Alvin was desperate. A knee to his crotch wasn't going to hinder him for long.

I kept my eyes on him as I backed toward the corridor. Effie took my arm and pressed the strap of my purse into my hand. I grabbed hold of it like a lifeline. Under my breath, I said, "We've got to make a run for it. Can you do it?"

"Yes, dear."

We were almost to the opening when Alvin straightened up. His face was twisted with pain that was underlined with rage. His mouth formed words, but I didn't stick around to find out what they were.

"Go!" I said.

Effie was off like a rocket that unfortunately was missing most of its firing power. I slowed my pace, so I wouldn't dislocate her shoulder as I towed her along. Loping down the corridor, I cast about for some way to stop Alvin or at least slow him down. We needed time to get to the entrance, where I hoped Bailey would be out and about looking for me.

The cut on my arm ached. My head throbbed. I had no weapon. I had Effie hanging on one side of me, while my handbag weighed me down on the other. Filled with frustration, I struck the purse with my fist and hit the container of flower preservative.

We rounded the first bend of the corridor and our movement activated the sensor that turned on the ball of hot light. Effie gasped. "I can't see."

"Close your eyes. I'll lead the way. It's only a short distance, and then the light will go out."

I chewed my lower lip. Effie's words, "I can't see," had given me an idea. But would it work?

Swiftly, I went over the design of the corridor. After the glaring light came Tornado Alley. The winds were fierce, and if I was positioned right, I had the makings of a sandstorm in my purse.

Behind us, Alvin shouted, "I'm going to get you, Bretta."

"Not if I get you first," I muttered. I unzipped my purse and took out the plastic pint of flower preservative. It was a weak ploy, but it might gain us enough time to get out of the cave.

We moved past the sensors, and the glaring light dimmed.

For a brief moment, darkness wrapped us in a false sense of security. Then I heard Alvin. He was closing in.

If my plan was to work, Effie and I had to get through tornado alley very quickly. The TORNADO ALLEY sign flashed on. The air began to flow, gaining momentum. I ignored the pictures that were projected on the ceiling and walls, and hustled Effie through the technical-wrought storm.

Once we cleared the sensors the sign flashed off. The wind died. I glanced behind me. The ball of light illuminated the corridor with its harsh glow.

I urged Effie over to the wall and whispered, "Cover your face, and don't look around until I tell you. Okay?"

"What are you going to do?"

"No time. Trust me."

"Without a doubt, dear."

I left my purse on the floor so both of my hands were free. I uncapped the flower preservative. The white powder was smaller than grains of sand. If I gauged my action correctly, if Alvin unwittingly cooperated, I could empty the container, and the whirlwind would do the rest. But first I had to find a place to stand where he wouldn't see me. The element of surprise had to be on my side.

The only source of light was the TORNADO ALLEY sign that came on when movement was detected. With that in mind, I shifted to my far right and pressed my face against the cold stone. Anxiety built in my chest. Where was Alvin? The ball of light had long since dimmed. He should have activated the TORNADO ALLEY sign by now. I tried to still my breathing. What was he waiting for?

A gentle breeze touched my hot cheeks. The air jets kicked in. The sign flashed on. I turned and saw Alvin at the same moment he saw me. He charged. I tossed the powder into the air. Instantly, the grit was sucked up by the wind and flung in all directions.

I quickly covered my face, but still felt the sting. Alvin squealed like a pig, but I didn't look. I grabbed Effie's arm.

She reached up and touched my cheek with trembling fingers. "That was damned resourceful, dear. You're one hell of a florist."

Effie was taken to a local hospital for a thorough examination and kept for observation to make sure her ordeal hadn't put her health at risk. She didn't attend the contest, and I barely made it myself. I'd changed out of my wet clothes, and had received eight stitches to the cut on my arm. The wound ached, but at ten after ten, I took my place before a room filled with eager florists impatient to get the competition under way.

Reggie and the Missouri Highway Patrol had taken Alvin into custody after his eyes had been cleansed. Bailey had stayed behind to take my statement. I'd given him a quick rundown of events, and then had excused myself to conduct the contest.

Bailey stood at the back of the room, his arms folded over his chest, his chin set at an angle that rocked my concentration. I forced my gaze away from him and to the four contestants—Robbee, Miriam, Chloe, and Zach. I smiled with what I hoped might be taken as confidence, though I hadn't an ounce.

When Effie had walloped Alvin with my purse, the impact of the blow had shattered the compact disc case, scratching a deep groove on the playing surface. That CD had been the contest. I'd worked hard finding songs with flowers in the titles—

"Days of Wine and Roses." "Tiptoe Through the Tulips." "You Don't Bring Me Flowers Anymore." "Cherry Pink and Apple Blossom White." Each tune had been recorded on the disk, and would've given the contestants adequate time to interpret their own rendition into a bouquet.

As the applause died away, I risked another glance at Bailey. In the excitement of giving my statement, I'd told him that the "key" to the contest had been ruined. He'd bitten back the "if you'd mind your own business" lecture, saying that something would come to me. Of all the people in the room, only he understood the task I faced at bluffing my audience into thinking I knew what I was doing.

I made eye contact with Bailey, and an unexpected peace came over me. I relaxed my tense shoulders. "Good morning. My name is Bretta Solomon. Welcome to Branson and to our contest."

I paused when out of the corner of my eye I saw Bailey reach into his pocket for his phone. He listened briefly. As he returned the shiny gadget to his jacket, he looked straight at me, nodded, and then headed for the door.

My heart skipped a beat. Was he off on another assignment? Didn't he get a rest before he started a new case? But the real source of my agitation came from the fact that he was leaving.

I searched my brain for a parting remark that only Bailey might understand. When I spoke, I heard the smile in my voice. "The title of the first category in our competition is 'Butterflies and Flowers—the right combination.' "

The contestants stared as if I'd lost my mind. Bailey stopped and turned in my direction. He touched his lips with his index finger, then pointed that finger at me. "Soon," he mouthed, then he walked from the room.

I wanted more, but for now, that would have to be enough. I faced the contestants. "To enjoy life you have to live it. Bloom where you're planted, ladies and gentlemen. Take a lesson from the lovely butterfly. Ride the air currents, and let your imagination soar."